Electric Alien Passion

by Sharon Barrington

Shelbi MacPhadden Adventure 3

Published by:

ESIL Publishing,
638 Buchan Avenue, Oshawa, ON, Canada, L1J 3A3

The characters and situations portrayed in this book are fictional. Any resemblance to persons living or dead is purely coincidental.

This book contains an excerpt from the forthcoming book, *Warrior Alien Passion* by Sharon Barrington. This excerpt has been developed for this edition only and may not reflect the final version of the forthcoming book.

Barrington, Sharon

ISBN: 978-0-9683356-9-7

Copyright © 2018 by ESIL

Excerpt from *Warrior Alien Passion* by Sharon Barrington Copyright © 2019 by ESIL

Cover design by Melody Simmons <u>bookcoverscre8tive.com</u>

Table of Contents

Dear Reader,

Thank you for downloading my book, ELECTRIC ALIEN PASSION.

I hope it will make you smile, give you a sensual moment, or some warm personal feelings as you join Shelbi MacPhadden on her next journey to a new alien world of delightful, passionate lovemaking.

Sit down, lie back, or enjoy it wherever you feel free and comfortable to read and be stimulated for the sheer joy of sweet, physical, passionate sex.

If this story brought a smile to your lips, or a thrill to any part of your body, or just a moment of sexual fantasy and lovemaking, then I have made a small difference in your life. To me, that is a great feeling and why I write these stories.

Here's to your personal excitement and passion!

Sharon Barrington

Chapter 1: War Ready

Lieutenant Shelbi MacPhadden's spaceship, the Gryphon, dropped out of hyperspace and disappeared in seven nano seconds. She sat warrior alert in her command chair inside her fully armed space suit, ready for anything.

Her Command Life Capsule (CLC) enclosed the spacesuit covering her shapely human body. It was built specifically for her curves and could sustain a direct laser missile hit. Even if the ship disintegrated around her, the CLC would still support her life system for up to three months in cold space hibernation.

As the ship travelled through hyperspace, she laid her tired head in her upturned palms. She was weary from reading all the background information on the new Planet Cirtece and strategizing how to stay safe.

Her empire directive from Commander Clive Bondwin had ordered her to Planet Cirtece to build relationships with the business people and defend the planet if necessary from the totalitarian enemy, Coalition Sergoymils. Several of their coalition stealth scout ships were registered in the outer reaches of this galaxy.

When Shelbi dropped out of hyperspace, she would be safe or fighting for her life.

When her empire commander commissioned her to go to the new world, it had been on an amber grade two alert. She was aware this could have turned to a red grade one alert with enemies waiting for her arrival while she was in hyperspace.

"No good being eliminated before I even play the game," she said aloud.

Shelbi continued to scroll through the background information on these aliens on the data cube. She found one interesting fact. They had unusual eye lens properties that allowed them to see unique electric colours swirling around their bodies like a personal aura that shifted depending on their mood or activities. Shelbi wondered what it would be like to see her own electric aura, especially when making love.

Shelbi moved to her bedroom as she continued her hyperspace journey and thought back to why she became part of the empire's warrior princess elite group. The empire had specifically created the group to be the military strategic elite and the relationship builders between Earth's empire culture and any new planets they encountered as they expanded through the universe.

While growing up on Earth, she enjoyed being a girl and playing with toys. As her body and mind grew, she began to play more games with the other children using computers and special military team war games.

By the time Shelbi was 13, she had a special space uniform moulded just for her that adjusted as she grew through her teenage years. It fitted tightly to her body as it filled out to accommodate her broadening hips and her growing breasts.

Shelbi's first application to be a warrior princess was accepted gratefully by the empire warrior scout who had been tracking her progress. She was awarded the honour of joining the empire's warrior princess elite program at the academy three months after her 19th birthday, just months after becoming eligible.

As she continued that night on her hyperspace voyage, she thought back to the war games in her graduation year when she was teamed up with Cadet Phillip Yerffej from Cirtece.

Before she met him, she had read in the academy background documents about the impact imperfect radiation shielding had during the first space voyage from Earth to their new home on Cirtece many years ago. Now, all the men and women from Cirtece had hair of differing brown shades. The males had dark green eyes with black flecks and females had light green eyes with blue flecks.

Because the gravity of the planet they landed on was only 80% of Earth's, they grew taller than humans did. The average Cirtece male was six foot seven with broad shoulders, firm biceps, and a broad chest. The females were six foot one on average and had broad shoulders, larger breasts than Earth's humans, and long slim legs tapering from broad hips on an hourglass waist, the equivalent of a size 18.

When she saw Phillip at the empire war games meeting, she knew of his size but was not ready for the sheer force of electric energy he brought into the room. It was breath-taking, in a good way. His large hand reached out and engulfed her hand gently. He shook it firmly but with a control that let her know he could just as easily crush the hand of an enemy. The electric sparks that rushed up her arm set her skin on fire. Her mind thought of his naked arm curled around her pale body.

"Control," she said under breath. "Shelbi, this is war games not sex athletics."

Phillip was not ready for the electric energy Shelbi fired up his muscular arm either. He was used to the energy pulsating from women on his planet but not alien women from Earth, especially not ones with copper red hair. His mind slipped from its warrior stance, wondering, *"Does she have red hair in other places?"*

In the war games, their sexual tension was replaced with the tension of combat battle. As professionals, they fought side by side on a new planet for four days. When they finished, the sexual tension and attraction of their well-honed bodies rose up to a higher level.

On the third night, after spending two hours talking strategy sitting beside Phillip, she had been so wet between her legs that she was afraid to stand up in case it showed through her uniform pants. She had quickly walked to her bedroom and swiftly closed the door.

Lying naked on the bed, her hands roamed over her ample pale breasts, cupping and squeezing them seductively. Her fingers began to circle her pink nipples and made each one tense and pert. As the tingling spread down her body, she began to pluck at each stiffing nipple urgently.

Her hands began moving across her firm curvy hips and stroked the soft skin on her outer thighs. Then she spread her legs and moved her hands to her soft inner core. Finally, panting, she ran her fingers up and down her pouting, tingling vagina lips. Thinking about Phillip's huge manhood made her wet and the moisture dripped from her throbbing vagina.

"Oh, can I really take his full manhood?" she spoke aloud to her empty room as she plunged one, then two, then three of her fingers urgently in and out of her wet, hot vagina. Pushing them past her engorged vagina lips, she tried to stretch herself and imagine the sweet sexual pain of him slowly entering her. She vividly imagined him pushing deeper and deeper inside her as she clung to his broad shoulders with her nipples pressed against his hard, hot abs.

***

Phillip was in a similar state in his bedroom. He wanted her so much but was concerned about whether she could stretch to take his full manhood in her small, almost petite human vagina. He had never made love to a human from Earth but he knew they were smaller than females on his planet. Still, he wanted her so much.

He understood how to be gentle with women. He knew how to make love with some sexy sweetness and a little enticing pain. He would never hurt a woman. As a Cirtece noble person, a fact he never told anyone at the empire academy, his personal credo was to protect women at all costs.

As he continued to stroke his rock-hard rod, he thought of her naked beside him and kissing her pink nipples until they were pert and she arched her soft white back in sexual tension.

"It would feel so great to pillow my face in her soft creamy breasts!" he exclaimed aloud now in full passion.

As his manly sexual tension mounted and he could see his body's red and yellow electric aura rise, he revelled in his graphic thoughts. He imagined stripping all her clothes off, and then kissing her beautiful, pale, naked body softly all the way to the copper mound above her sensual curvy thighs. Just thinking of rubbing his lips in her curly copper hair and inhaling her sexy womanly scent made his cock ache.

He stroked his manhood faster as be imagined her pale legs spread before him and the pouting red lips of her wet vagina. He thought about running his tongue up her inner soft thighs and arriving at the sweetness of her womanhood. He could almost taste her sexual juices as they flowed into his mouth. He longed to run his tongue over her erect, sensitive clitoris until she begged for his manhood inside her.

He knew he would have to be very patient and careful not to ever hurt her, but that would not stop him wanting to enter and stretch her wet vagina until he spurted his manly juices. This drove him to his own climax as his alien juices spurted from his long rod.

***

They were sent to the farthest empty planet in the war games galaxy zone on the fourth day. They arrived and began executing their plan to secure their target. It never happened.

As they were hiking in their non-spacesuit gear to the three-mile turning point, a flashing message arrived on their helmet coms. Two rogue Sergoymils teams had unsheathed their scout ships and landed nearby. Clearly, they wanted to capture them and steal the empire's technologically advanced war equipment.

They nearly missed the cold, calculating Sergoymils teams attacking, but the Sergoymils did not know what they were up against with these two empire elite warriors. Then their world exploded all around them as the second Sergoymils team tried to bury them in the grey soil. Showing the patience of a warrior, Phillip covered Shelbi first with his body then rolled her over of the edge of the grey sandy crater. Shelbi came up and spotted the Sergoymils team now, with the typical overconfidence of their species, advancing on them in the open desert.

Shelbi's first shot split the first Sergoymils member in two and Phillip's simultaneous gunshot exploded the head of the second one. In seconds, all four Sergoymils members had gone to join their alien maker.

Then the throbbing pain in her left knee began. She had twisted her knee during the fighting, but the adrenaline and her focus had masked the pain.

Phillip felt the electrical short of her body flow before Shelbi did. He dropped down beside her and looked into her pained eyes. They were four miles from the ship and she was down. There might be other Sergoymils warriors in the area. He made a split-second decision for the one he loved.

"Shelbi, I can help you," Phillip whispered, "but you can never tell anyone how I did this."

"Yes, Phillip. It's a deal," she said through clenched teeth.

"Shelbi, I am a Naykin healer on my planet, but I have never tried this with your species before. I don't know if it will work, but it will not hurt." Phillip continued, "I use my body, mind, and the electrical waves of the universe to heal you. This works on the physical side of the injury and on the part of your mind where pain lies."

The pain was settling into Shelbi's tired body. She looked into his green eyes and softly said, "Phillip, you are my warrior friend and perhaps more if that is what the universe has planned. I trust you to help me and not hurt me ever. Please do what you can now."

Her last words pushed all caution out of Phillip's mind. He pushed the tabs on her combat suit's left side to release her pale thigh. He immediately saw her twisted leg and swollen knee. Phillip shed his black jacket and blue t-shirt while calming his mind. His bare brown muscular arms reached out and his huge hands hovered over her swollen knee.

She gazed up into his eyes, seeking relieve.

His eyes never left Shelbi's crystal blue orbs.

Then she felt engulfed in his aura. The electricity was a charge like nothing she had felt in any surgical operation or healing process before. The warmth in her knee spread to her leg, which slid straight. The swelling in her knee slowly disappeared. The pain ebbed like a warm wave flowing out to sea.

"Oh, Phillip," she gasped. "That feels amazing."

Then the electricity hit her brain with a wave of red tingling heat. Almost painful, it rolled around her skull and focused her whole attention on its source: Phillip's mind.

Phillip was swaying and his electrical aura now, pulsating between them. He tried to let go. The electrical energy hit Shelbi like nothing she had experienced before. Then the strangest thing happened.

She could hear his thoughts.

His thoughts rolled over her mind. *"Oh no, we are mind bonding. This has never been done with a non-Cirtece before! What have I done?"*

Shelbi reached up automatically and gently placed her left hand on the back of his muscular, sweating neck. She felt the flow of electricity dance over her skin. His body rolled away from Shelbi's half-sitting form, breaking the electrical sensation surrounding their bodies.

"Are you all right?" he asked.

Shelbi shuddered, *"My knee is fine, almost better than before."*

"But your mind," he quickly asked, *"how is your mind?"*

"My mind is humming a little but feels fine. The pain is like a small buzz. I feel a calm mental energy that I have never felt before."

To their amazement and excitement, they both realized that they had not said a word aloud. It had all been linked in their heads.

***

She paused remembering all this history and wondering if she would find him on the planet when she arrived.

Now Shelbi heard the ship's urgent tone calling for her attention. She was still in stealth mode. The Gryphon had released nano drone probes in irregular waves to confuse the enemy. They would appear as debris on any enemy search.

Sitting warrior still, she focused on the data stream coming though on the face screen within her space suit. The information came back and her tech Special Program Elite Intelligence Management (SPEIM) analyzed it quickly. The enemy Coalition Sergoymils appeared to have no permanent inhabitants, ports, or spacecraft in this universe; nothing permanent had been created. That didn't mean they had no stealth vehicles though.

After all this combat tension, she needed some really athletic sex with a strong sweating alien man to play with her hot body and kiss her soft eager breasts while entering her warm moist vagina, again and again and again.

With those delicious thoughts on her mind, she set a course for Cirtece.

Chapter 2: A Signature Dress for a Princess Warrior

As part of her elite training, Shelbi had learned one of the ways to integrate into an alien culture was to discover more about their arts. A second key factor was to support their charities and galas. What was on her mind today was getting to know some clothing designers to help her with an outfit for an upcoming gala.

She found that, like many cultures, the people of this world enjoyed getting dressed up for parties. When Shelbi learned that Keith and Susan were key sponsors for the Tenju Gala, she immediately asked if she could be part of it. In further conversations with Susan, she had learned that this gala required men and women to dress formally.

Shelbi had asked Susan to suggest a young, up-and-coming designer who could create a signature dress for this first major event she was to attend. Susan was very plugged into the designer market and immediately identified Ricardo Berrel who she felt could be a major worldwide designer with some support. She had worn several of his dresses at balls and galas and not only found them spectacular but amazingly comfortable to wear for such long evenings.

Susan told her, "I think I should tell you that when he designs his dresses, he likes you to be nude to understand how all the parts of your body flow, how the electrical energy lights up various parts of your body, your hips, your breasts. Then he designs a dress in the fabric that he thinks will show your body off at its best."

Shelbi tilted her head back and laughed. "Susan, that is not a problem. If that's the way he designs dresses, it should be an interesting experience."

Several days later, she found herself driving up to an amazing silver-grey, stone architectural building. The grounds exuded the energy of nature and created excitement simply driving past the various colourful red, yellow, and green bushes. The glass of the building made optimum use of the sunlight entering and created an inviting entrance.

She parked her car and walked up the broad pale red granite steps toward the double amber glass doors. They automatically opened as she neared and she walked into the warm reception area. A well-dressed young woman stepped forward and said, "Good afternoon, Lieutenant MacPhadden. It is our pleasure to have you here."

Shelbi was slightly taken aback at the formal approach. "Thank you very much. I'm looking forward to an interesting time," she said with a smile.

"Hopefully it will be both interesting and enjoyable, Lieutenant MacPhadden. My name is Lisa Satswich and I will be your host for this design appointment. Please follow me and I can introduce you to Ricardo Berrel and his team."

Shelbi walked beside her down a short pale blue corridor and toward another set of large double redwood doors that opened into a small reception area. Lisa kept walking through the next set of double white wooden doors so Shelbi followed. As she walked into the next room, she thought it felt warmer than the rest of the building.

A tall, broad-shouldered man with dark hair flowing down to his shoulders walked towards her purposely.

"Hello Lieutenant MacPhadden. I'm Ricardo! Welcome to my design studio. Would you like anything to drink? Water, sparkling water, tea, coffee, or something stronger?"

Ricardo tilted his head slightly to the side as he spoke. Shelbi glanced at his broad shoulders and the strong sculptured muscles shaping each arm. She then noticed the amazing green patterned shirt that seemed to flow over his body while showing off the broad planes of his chest and the rippling muscles of his forearms. It set off his dark green eyes, making them intense and focused but not uncomfortably so.

"I'm fine, thank you very much," she said. "At least for the moment. Let's see how things go as we work together."

"Wonderful," Ricardo said. "Let me explain how we would like to work with you this afternoon. I believe," his rich baritone voice rolled out, "Susan has explained to you that in order for me to design what I think is the most fabulous dress in the world for you, I need to watch your body movements. I ask that you take off your clothes and be prepared to walk around naked. If you're not comfortable with that, I can supply you with a small thong and coverings for your nipples. This allows me to visualize and understand exactly how your body flows and how the energy colours light up your body's movements. Then I can design a dress to enhance those movements, not restrict them. I can take advantage of your natural electrical energy."

He paused clearly waiting for Shelbi to respond.

Shelbi smiled softly and said, "I think it will be interesting and I'm looking forward to it. I've heard about the electric colours you're talking about, but I've never seen them myself. Anyway, I've been naked in front of my doctor, naked in front of other warriors, and naked in front of my lovers. Being naked in front of you and your designers is another experience I believe I will enjoy."

His head tilted back slightly and a warm, rich laugh emerged from his lips. "That's just wonderful," he said. "I like a strong woman who knows exactly what she can do and how she will feel in any circumstance. Shelbi, I also want you to be aware that we will be digitally recording all your movements. The tape will be held in a secure computer bank that has no outside access whatsoever. I need to be able to review your video as I design the dress and use some holographic design software I've created to see how the fabric will flow naturally from your hips and breasts. Do you have a problem with that?"

Shelbi answered, "If it helps the design process, I'm fine with it."

"I'd like to introduce you to my co-designers. This is Sandy Fenwick," he said as he turned toward a young gentleman wearing a well-tailored shirt and jacket that did nothing to hide his strong muscular arms as he strode forward with his hand out.

"Lieutenant Shelbi, it's an honour to meet you," he said with a voice that was husky and manly.

"It's a pleasure to meet you, Sandy," Shelbi said slightly breathlessly.

Ricardo then waved to a young woman with blonde hair with ribbons of pale blue through it. Shelbi walked over to her while Ricardo said, "This is Joanne Stratton Cliffton who has also been with me for several years. She provides just the right touch of cosmetics, perfumes, and other feminine insights into the flow of garments."

The young woman strode up to Shelbi. She wore well-tailored beige pants that seemed to glide with each step and showed off her wonderful long, slim legs. The soft yellow blouse she was wearing flowed across her full breasts and seemed to accent them erotically. Joanne stretched out her hand.

"Lieutenant Shelbi, it's a pleasure to meet you," she said with warmth.

"Joanne, the pleasure is mutual. Before we get started, perhaps the three of you could give me a little insight into your backgrounds."

Sandy spoke up first. "As the newbie, I will start. I have lived all my life in this wonderful city and have never been off planet, but I have had the pleasure of being involved with a number of wonderful people from various planets and parts of this world. I started doing art and colour work when I was very young. When I saw Ricardo's designs, I thought I must work for the man. I must learn how he makes those amazing fabrics flow and accent the body. So, being a brash art student, I put together an art portfolio and waylaid Ricardo in the parking lot of this studio one morning. He took pity on me and asked me inside for a cup of coffee. We have worked together ever since."

Shelbi said with a smile, "Interesting. Clearly, he saw the special side of your designs and made a quick command decision. Good for you, Sandy."

Joanne, who had sat down on a wooden stool, spoke up next. "I was working at a design show for new designers doing their first clothing lines. When I saw the models and the clothes they were wearing designed by Ricardo, I felt I just had to be part of that excitement every day I went to work. Ricardo had a young girl as part of his model set who had some unfortunate markings on her arms. I was able to work my colour magic and make them appealing rather than a distraction."

Ricardo jumped in enthusiastically, "Yes, actually Joanne has the ability to use a few colours to turn parts of the body into moving imagery. She is truly amazing."

Joanne blushed as Ricardo spoke. She was clearly almost embarrassed when her mentor gave her such high praise.

Shelbi spoke up next. "Thank you. Ricardo and I had a discussion last week so he was kind enough to give me his background then. I have to tell you I'm very excited about this opportunity."

Sandy then looked Shelbi square in her crystal blue eyes and asked almost sternly, "Why do you want to wear a dress designed by Ricardo?"

All eyes turned to Shelbi. "I want to support the Tenju Gala since I believe any effort to assist orphan children on any planet should be supported. I want to make a statement to show that support and not just attend the event," Shelbi said and then paused looking around at the group. "Why Ricardo? Because Susan showed me some of his dress designs. I felt they were elegant, sexy, revealing, astonishing, and beautiful all at the same time. I wanted to know what it was like to go through his design experience. I wanted to wear an elegant garment that I've seen look so amazing on other females. I wanted to feel the fabric that Ricardo's dresses were made of touching my bare skin all over my body. I wanted to see how a dress can create its own electricity and glow."

Looking directly at Ricardo then scanning the group Shelbi continued, "I want to support Ricardo and all your careers because I feel your designs go beyond mere clothing. They are an expression of the character of the person wearing them. More women need that in their lives. A magnificent signature dress at this gala will help send that message."

Sandy tilted her head, smiled and said, "Wow, it is amazing to hear someone who gets what we are trying to do. You just put the design bar higher to create a special dress for you. Thanks for the challenge!"

Ricardo turned to Shelbi smiling and said, "It's time to take you to the dressing room so you can get prepared."

As Shelbi walked through the studio, she noted that it felt quite warm. She thought, *"He's turned the heat up in the studio so I won't feel cold walking around. Excellent! My cherry nipples will stand to attention with all this excitement. It should be good for designing how the dress fabric will really fall."*

She entered a room with a full set of mirrors covered one wall. Another side supported a table with more mirrors around that were clearly for makeup. A large shower filled the left corner. The glass around it was tinted and coloured and seemed to move.

She walked into the centre of the room. Ricardo entered carrying a box. He handed it to her. The grey box had a large blue satin bow and ribbon around it. Her name had been printed on the box in beautiful handwriting. Ricardo spoke in his deep masculine voice, "I'd like you to accept this present. It's something you can wear today and be comfortable in, I hope."

Shelbi pulled the blue satin bow, opened the pearl-coloured lid, and parted the soft pale-yellow tissue paper. When she pulled the garment out, she saw it was a beautiful kimono robe made from some wonderful fabric she'd never felt before, but was similar to silk back on Earth. The colours were blue, purple, and mauve and seemed to have a movement all of their own.

"Shelbi, I designed it specifically for you for this day. Please accept it is a gift that you can wear whenever you want," Ricardo remarked.

"Thank you very much, Ricardo. What an amazing kimono. I really appreciate this gift," Shelbi said, slightly awed at the magnificent colourful garment.

Lisa placed Shelbi's bag on the floor and said, "If you could disrobe now and come out barefoot and nude, we can start the design session. Also, please pick out two or three pairs of high-heeled shoes you've brought that you would feel comfortable wearing later. Ricardo likes his clients to wear them so we can see how the muscles in the back of the leg and thigh react just as they will at the gala when walking or dancing. Simply leave them on the floor and we will get them later."

Shelbi thought back to her words, *"Naked in front of my doctor, naked in front of other warriors, and naked with my lovers. OK, time to get naked in front of these intense designers."*

When she put on the kimono for the first time and felt the fabric against her naked skin, she felt almost erotic. Electricity seemed to flow over her body. She thought, *"Shelbi, stay in control. This feels so wonderful, but you are here for dress design purposes, not to climax in front of a group of artistic professionals."*

Walking out barefoot, she again appreciated the warmth of the room. All three designers turned and seemed to devour her with their eyes as she walked forward, her ivory legs showing.

She walked up to Ricardo, slipped her kimono off, and handed it to him. He passed it to Sandy who turned around, put it on a wooden hanger, and hung it up.

"Whenever you want the kimono back, just ask," Sandy whispered so as not to break the mood.

Ricardo asked Shelbi to stand still as the three designers walked around her naked body in different directions.

Sandy dropped down and seemed to stare at the bottom of her bare legs and feet at one point. She ran her left hand over the bare skin of Shelbi's left thigh to feel the curves and flow of her form. Joanne came forward with some colour wheels and put them next to the creamy skin of her hips. Then she stared at the red hair on her head. Shelbi felt like a human object of interest.

Ricardo then said, "Shelbi, I'd like you to walk around so we can see how your body parts naturally move and flow. We want to understand how your leg muscles shape up, your breasts move, and your arms sway."

Shelbi began to walk around and felt she was being a little stiff.

Sandy spoke up, "Lieutenant Shelbi."

Shelbi held up her right hand. "Given I'm the one who's naked here, I think we can dispense with the lieutenant part. Please call me Shelbi for the rest of the day," Shelbi said with a warm smile.

Both Sandy and Joanne looked at each other and seemed slightly uneasy about that approach to a client. Ricardo filled in the gap by warmly saying, "Wonderful, let's call you Shelbi just for today then. Thank you for being so open."

Shelbi would later learn that many of the people in this culture never allowed the designers to call them by their first name. A silly notion that let them think they had the upper hand.

Shelbi wanted him to design a dress that showed her body in the best possible way. She wanted to begin the intimate feeling that would lead to being on a first name basis.

After about a half an hour of having her walk around in bare feet and do some stretching, arm movements, and posing, Ricardo asked Sandy and Joanne to fetch several pairs of high-heeled shoes.

Shelbi put the first pair of black suede shoes on and noticed how they pulled her naked thigh muscles and the backs of her naked pale legs tighter.

Ricardo asked Shelbi, "Please walk around as you did before."

As Shelbi was walking and not really focusing, Ricardo broke her trance with a question. "Do your nipples always become red and pert when you walk?"

"Only when I'm excited, Ricardo," she said with a smile as she gazed down at her coned red nipples. "I guess all this walking around nude is more erotic than I thought," she added as she laughed.

He then switched her over to slightly higher heeled shoes and again watched her walk around.

Ricardo suggested, "I think we should take a break and have some light refreshments. Does that sound like a good idea, Shelbi?"

"Absolutely! I didn't realize I was beginning to feel a little tired."

Joanne helped Shelbi into her soft kimono and then walked over to a small area with comfortable beige wooden chairs with soft cushions on the bottom and back. There was also a table laid out with enough food for a small army. Shelbi grabbed a tall crystal glass and poured some sparkling water into it. She drank thirstily and then sat down in a large beige armchair.

Ricardo looked thoughtful then spoke up, looking her directly in the eyes, "Shelbi, I'd like to have you dance so we can see how you move. I can call a wonderful dancer to be your partner. However, I would still like you to dance nude with just your shoes on. Does that sound like a good idea or . . ."?

Shelbi looked him straight in the face. "Ricardo, you're the designer. If that's going to help you create one of your amazing signature dresses for me, done!"

Sandy moved off and made a call. About 20 minutes later, Shelbi felt refreshed and ready to go. There was a brief commotion as a tall, well-built man walked into the room. He was slightly shorter than Ricardo, but had similar well-sculpted body features. The new man also had wonderful black hair that flowed to his broad, muscular shoulders. His beautiful dark green eyes were filled with soft affection yet stern at the same time. His chiselled facial features showed the exercise level of a professional dancer. He walked with graceful motion across the room, with his large right hand outstretched.

"Lieutenant Shelbi, may I have this dance?" he said with a hint of laughter in his voice.

Ricardo jumped out of his seat. "Shelbi, let me introduce you to Louis. He is an average dancer."

Louis laughed and reached over to smack Ricardo on the shoulder. "Typical, you need my services more than I need to be here, and thank you for the compliment."

It was clear there was a great deal of camaraderie between these two men. Later, Shelbi would learn that Louis was actually Ricardo's younger brother, and a world-class professional dancer. Fortunately, she did not know that at the time or she would have been intimidated since dancing was not her strong point.

Louis held out his right hand and Shelbi shook it. She was pleasantly surprised by how gentle and warm it was.

"Well, Louis, if I'm going to be naked and dancing with you, the least you could do is take off your shirt," she said with a hint of laughter in her voice.

Louis laughed heartily. "A lady with a sense of humour! How wonderful!"

As he began to unbutton his shirt, Shelbi realized she may have made a strategic error. Louis's chest was covered in fine curly black hair. As his powder blue shirt slid off his muscular toned arms, she saw there was a power in them that would help her on the dance floor. Her mind returned to his hairy chest and her pink nipples began to get harder. She thought, *"My nipples are going to rub against him and I'm going to have to work on holding myself back. If I get wet, it will drip down my legs, and that would not be good!"*

Shelbi slipped off her kimono, put on a pair of blue high-heeled shoes, and walked out on to the redwood floor of the studio. Ricardo followed her, as did Sandy and Joanne. Louis did a little stretching before he walked up to her. He slipped off his shoes and stood barefoot and bare chested in front of the nude Shelbi.

Louis reached out and put his hand on her naked thigh. She felt the warmth there. However, it was clear this was a business situation and not a lover's first caress.

"Louis, I bet you're this gentle with all the ladies," Shelbi said.

Louis spoke up quickly, "I am, especially when the dancer in my arms is my wife. Or a warrior princess that could cause great pain if I did the wrong thing."

The smile on his face showed he was just having fun and not really worried about Shelbi being a killer warrior.

He had set the tone so Shelbi could relax and realize this really was a business situation and that Louis was there to support Ricardo and to help her. She knew the fact she was naked was merely part of the design situation, not anything he found erotic.

She was not quite right.

Louis thought, *"I really have to be careful here. She needs my support and not a lustful young man. She has such a magnificent body with alabaster skin, those wide hips, and soft shoulders. It's a blessing that I married my wonderful wife and can focus on thinking about her while we are dancing."*

The next hour was spent with Shelbi and Louis dancing slow and fast. As she suspected, her nipples kept rubbing against the wiry black hairs of his manly chest. He seemed to sense her emotions. Just when she was worried that her nipples were too tense, he pulled her into his body. The warmth of his body relaxed them slightly. However, the erotic sensuality kept rolling through her body in various stages. The heat between her legs was only cooled by being naked.

"God, I hope I don't get really wet," she thought, but then her Princess training came into play and her control over her emotions and some of her body functions kicked in. Later, when she lay in bed and thought about Phillip, her hot juices could flow.

Louis was also struggling. The rise of hot feelings was evident by his manhood hardening. He just kept his focus on the dance steps, arching his back, maintaining his stance. *"Her body is so soft and small it must be so exciting to caresses that ivory skin. Those strawberry pink nipples are just ripe for plucking."* All these thoughts flooded his mind as they danced a slow waltz. *"Focus, focus on the steps, the dance pattern. I can get through this without embarrassing Shelbi or myself. Sure I can!"* he told himself.

As they continued to dance, they both found a rhythm that worked for their bodies. They sensed each other's reactions, but both were professionals. They needed to perform their duty for Ricardo and his team, not give into their simmering lust.

"Shelbi, you've been a wonderful model. I really have much more than I hoped," Ricardo said as his face lit up. "Your body is very toned but still has an amazing rhythm and flow. Your legs have an amazing silhouette. The electric colour flowing around your body is amazing. Your breasts have a unique rhythm that has given me wonderful design thoughts for the fabric I want to use."

She moved over to Louis, still nude, and stretched up on her toes to kiss his chiselled left cheek.

"Thank you for being a wonderful dance partner. You really added to the experience," Shelbi said with a smile on her lips.

"You're welcome," Louis said with a warm smile. "You are a wonderful dancer and I really enjoyed holding your naked body." He chuckled. "Shelbi, that really was fun for me. Thank you."

"We shall have to dance together at the gala with our clothes on just to be different," Shelbi laughed.

"Shelbi, it would be my pleasure to dance with you at the gala. Thank you for asking," Louis said with warmth in his voice.

Ricardo then said, "I've one more thing that we need to do today. I would like Joanne to accompany you back to the dressing room. She would like to try various cosmetic designs on your bare legs. The idea being that we can use them to enhance your legs and what the flow of the dress will reveal. Does that seem alright with you?"

Shelbi took a long sip of cool water and spoke, "Absolutely! This has been such an amazing design process. I am glad to do whatever you need."

Joanne and Lisa accompanied Shelbi back to the dressing room. Shelbi once more slipped off the kimono, which Lisa quickly took and folded back into the box that Ricardo had given her earlier. She wrapped the blue ribbon around it and left it for Shelbi to take home.

Shelbi had a quick wash under the warm shower to cleanse the perspiration from her body. She also cleaned the wetness from between her thighs. She walked over to Joanne as she dried herself with the soft beige terry towel.

Joanne began by running a warm cloth down her bare legs. Then she began to use various powders and colourings to enhance her thighs and her calves. When she finished doing one, Shelbi walked over and looked in the mirror. Her leg appeared to be moving even when she stood still. There was an energy flowing over her design on her skin. It was utterly amazing!

Joanne stopped after several more lower body cosmetic designs and felt she had enough to work with. Joanne and Lisa left Shelbi alone so she could shower again under the wonderful rainforest shower head to wash off the colourful designs.

As Shelbi walked out of the dressing room across the studio floor, with her gift under her arm, she saw that Ricardo was drawing on a great white board.

"Wow," she thought, *"he is already designing my gala dress. How wonderful!"*

The team stopped as Shelbi approached.

"How about one last drink before you go?" Ricardo asked.

"Great, but non-alcoholic since I am driving."

"Of course, sparkling citrus it is," Ricardo said.

When they all had a glass of the sparkling drink, Ricardo made a toast. "To one of the best client sessions we have ever had, and to one of the most pleasant clients we have ever designed a spectacular signature dress for. To Shelbi!"

"To Shelbi!" they all shouted together.

Then Shelbi held her glass up. "To an amazing experience with a wonderful professional group of artists."

Then nodding toward Louis, she raised her glass. "To a wonderful dance partner. To your health!"

"To his health!" they all shouted.

Thus ended one of Shelbi's more pleasant and emotional life experiences, until she was home and wrapped on her bed in her new kimono and her warm hands began caressing various parts of her body!

She began to think of Phillip and dancing with him as she had with Louis earlier that day, of Phillip's wonderful abs rippling as her red pert nipples rubbed against his manly brown chest. Her hands travelled down her pale stomach to the red mound above her wet inner thighs. She fantasised about his hot wet tongue caressing her vagina lips and tasting her sweetness. Her right hand travelled down her body and caressed her southern lips, building her excitement and tension. Finally, her long legs tensed, her pink pert nipples tingled, and the excitement rippled over her quivering thighs on to her flat stomach, and finally rolled over her bobbing ivory breasts.

"Phillip, Phillip, take me please!" she yelled aloud. "Take me any way you want, my love!"

Chapter 3: Showing Off Shelbi's Gala Body Art

The broad-shouldered, majestic male warrior was tense as he walked casually toward Shelbi's house. He surveyed the territory and made quick judgments about the terrain, escape routes, and any potential danger.

As he reached the magnificent redwood front door of Shelbi's house, he lifted a clenched fist. He knocked twice, paused, and then knocked once more.

Shelbi glanced up from her book, and smiled. *"The military love its secret codes no matter what the circumstance,"* she thought as she heard the knock combination on the wooden front door.

She walked to the door and felt the designer dress flutter against her body and thought how wonderful it felt softly caressing her outer thighs. Shelbi opened the door and, despite wearing five-inch heels making her over six feet tall, had to look up at the gentleman standing there.

"Lieutenant Sanders, what beautiful stars are out tonight," she said.

"And the stars are all in alignment," Lieutenant Sanders replied.

If Shelbi had not said beautiful, or Lieutenant Sanders had not said alignment, the mission would have been aborted. He would have moved quickly inside the door and shut it behind him. His training as a warrior prince elite made him the perfect candidate to escort Shelbi to the gala.

"Excuse me for a minute. I just need to grab some things before we leave," Shelbi said.

Lieutenant Sanders smiled and answered, "No problem, Lieutenant MacPhadden. Whenever you're ready."

Shelbi looked up at him and said, "Lieutenant, we're going to be together tonight at a public event. Please call me Shelbi. We don't really need the attention of a military title."

A deep-throated laugh filled with amusement emanated from him. "Wonderful, and please call me Paul."

Shelbi walked down the corridor and into her bedroom. She picked up her dangling diamond and jade earrings to hook into her soft pink ear lopes. Ricardo had specially designed them to fit as part of her gala ensemble. She then walked over to the dresser and picked up her dark blue and silver striped evening purse. Shelbi turned to glance once more in the full-length mirror. The soft midnight blue top showed her breasts off elegantly. The high collar caressed her soft white neck just below her red hair, styled for the gala. The full sleeves in the wonderful material flowed down her arms. She was amazed as she watched the soft blue skirt's material open to reveal her toned legs.

Purposefully, she pulled back the material to look at her magnificent long legs. Once again, she smiled and was inwardly amazed at how beautiful her tapered limbs looked, especially since the makeup had been applied so artfully.

"They look almost erotic with that unique flowing design. If Prince Phillip could only see my inner thighs now," she thought with a wicked smile across her red full lips.

Her mind slipped back to when Joanne had arrived from Ricardo's design studio with her makeup kit. She appeared very excited and energized as she met Shelbi at the front door.

"Shelbi MacPhadden, I would like to do a full lower body cosmetic makeup application for you!" she blurted out in her enthusiasm. "I know you will only be showing legs through the dress, but I'd like to have the opportunity to create a design you can feel to complete your look."

Shelbi smiled back and quickly answered, "That would wonderful. I've seen firsthand how beautiful your art is."

"Great. Not only will we do your legs inside and out, I will also do parts of your tummy, backside, and bare feet."

Shelbi had been warned by her sponsor Susan that Ricardo and his makeup designer would love to do full body makeup, but they had decided the legs were enough since the bottom half of the dress had long side slits and the rest of the dress hugged her body. Susan had asked Shelbi about the potential makeup designs to make sure they didn't violate any cultural boundaries. Shelbi assured Susan that this was not an issue.

Knowing what time Joanne was going to arrive, Shelbi had a hot shower, lathered up scented soap across her bare breasts, and shaved all the necessary body parts to be ready for whatever makeup was going to be applied.

Joanne had done some preliminary work at the design session weeks before. She also took samples of Shelbi's skin and blood to make sure that whatever cosmetics and oils she applied to her skin would not irritate her or cause health issues.

Shelbi was wearing the kimono that Ricardo had given her. She loved to wear it next to her bare skin as she felt it caress her, warm her, and comfort her. It was erotic and comforting at the same time.

The two women moved into Shelbi's large bathroom. Joanne put a red spongy mat on the floor for Shelbi to stand on. Shelbi had decided to take the kimono off and stood naked so Joanne could see her full body even though she was only doing the bottom part. She wanted her skin tones to be visible for this amazing artist. Shelbi knew she had electric colours around her body that the people of this planet could see but she could not.

Joanne could see Shelbi's electric aura. When she had first seen Shelbi naked at the dress design session, it had taken her breath away, not in a sexual or erotic way but in a wow-what-I-could-design-using-that-electric-colour-flow way. She would use it along with her specially created natural makeup to create a stunning effect that others could see and really appreciate.

Joanne looked at her original sketches and photographs and placed them on the floor outside the red mat area. She then took out her airbrushing equipment and went to work, starting on Shelbi's flat belly and around to her shapely smooth backside.

Joanne's airbrush and other brushes moved inches away from Shelbi's nude body. Her hands occasionally moved close and almost caressed her skin, but never seemed to touch it.

"Your electric aura colours are so amazing," Joanne mused, almost as if it was an inner thought.

She worked on creating imagery that would extend Shelbi's legs, create and heighten certain areas, and soften others. Shelbi watched the transformation, as she felt the warm spray flutter over her bare skin. Occasionally, she followed up an area with a long-handled soft blue bristle brush or a soft white wedge sponge. As she worked down her smooth stomach and began designing around and below her copper mound, Shelbi felt her emotions move from sensational to erotic. She had to pull her mind away as the warm spray caused hot sensations to begin to spread through her bare thighs and up her core.

Joanne was working on the inside of her thighs up near the lips of her now tingling sex. Shelbi sucked in her breath as the hot feeling went beyond erotic to spread across her stomach and tingle down her thighs.

"I really need to maintain a warrior stance," she thought.

As Joanne began to work on her right inner thigh, Shelbi asked if she could take a short break.

Joanne exclaimed, "I'm so sorry! I get so intense with my work that I forget how tired the people I'm working on must get."

Shelbi smiled warmly and looked at Joanne. "Actually, it's making me really horny. I have to stop and just gather my composure."

At first, Joanne looked horrified. Then Shelbi softly said, "It's a wonderful feeling but not really what I need when you're working on me. It's not your fault. It's just the way we humans are made."

Joanne quickly relaxed, knowing she had not offended Shelbi.

"Are your makeup colours waterproof?" Shelbi asked with a slight smile.

"Absolutely!" Joanne said. "We have the same juice flow challenge between our thighs as you do. So not to worry. In fact, I will add a special spray if you like to absorb some of the flow."

Shelbi nodded, as Joanne went back to rhythmic airbrushing, brushing, and sponging her body design.

When Joanne was finished, Shelbi stood naked in front of her full-length bedroom mirror and turned around and around and around. She was absolutely amazed at the rhythm the design created on her body. As she studied it, she saw the design between her thighs seemed to be deeper and almost mysterious. Her copper mound blended into the soft skin of her firm thighs. Her pale shapely hips appeared broader yet softer. Her long legs seemed longer and slimmer and a shimmering light rolled around them as she moved. Her pink bare feet also had a rhythm rolling across her toes and up her ankles.

Joanne had been watching her and appeared to be growing tense as the moments went on and Shelbi said nothing.

"Oh, One Mother, have I done a really bad job? Does she not like it? Oh, what is happening!" she thought, her furrowed brow growing more and more worried as the silence lingered on.

Shelbi turned to her with a full-on smile and the words exploded out of her mouth, "Joanne, this is the most amazing thing I have ever seen. You are truly a magnificent artist! I thank you for letting me wear your body art."

Joanne's eyes welled up with warm tears of joy. "Oh my gosh! Thank you so much. I'm so privileged to have had this opportunity. I am so happy you like it."

"I'm more than happy! I'm ecstatic! This is the most amazing transformation of a naked body I have ever experienced. You are going to be my new body makeup artist forever!"

Joanne closed her eyes and laughed heartily. "That's wonderful. I know this is new for you and I wasn't quite sure how you would accept it. You can't see your red and yellow electric aura, but I can. I really tried to capture the rhythms it has as the various colours roll around you. You look spectacular, even if I do say so myself."

Shelbi flashed back to the present and realized she'd been keeping Paul waiting. Still, she knew his military training meant he would patiently wait for her.

Lieutenant Sanders and Lieutenant MacPhadden strode out of Shelbi's house. They got into the blue stretch limousine and took the backward-facing seat to allow their sponsors to have the comfort of the forward-facing seat. The limo went down the wide tree-lined red asphalt driveway to pick up Keith and Susan, stopping at the front door of their magnificent house.

The housekeeper rushed out and opened the door.

"Lieutenant Shelbi!" she exclaimed. "Susan really wants to see your body design before you go to the gala. Please come in so she can have a quick look in private."

Shelbi laughed and got out of the limo. As she walked in, Susan excitedly rushed forward.

"I just have to see it, Shelbi! I've been on pins and needles all day wondering how you would feel about it, how you look, if you like it! Oh my gosh, this is so much fun!"

Shelbi laughed again. "Susan, relax. You'll burn up all the energy you need for the gala. I will tell you it was the most wonderful experience I've had with makeup in my life. Joanne is my new favourite makeup artist."

Susan clasped her hands together. "I'm so glad. I was so worried. We really didn't know enough about you to know if you would like or appreciate this kind of artwork. Come down to my private room so I can have a proper look," Susan said.

Susan motioned Shelbi into a room down a pale green hall. Then as Susan watched, Shelbi pulled back her dress showing her the outside skin of her right leg then her left then the inside skin of both legs. Susan was quiet.

Shelbi thought, *"Almost too quiet."*

Then Susan looked Shelbi directly in the eyes and said, "Joanne has done a wonderful design and you look stunning in it. If only you could see your electric aura and how it blends, rolls, and shimmers around the shadows and highlights of your legs. It is erotic. It is truly rich. It is simply elegant."

Susan pulled back her skirt on the right side and showed Shelbi what Joanne had done for her. Both women laughed. It was a unique experience shared between two people from different worlds, but so common for two women who are true friends.

Susan grabbed Shelbi's hand and said, "Quick, we must get to the Tenju Gala."

As the limo arrived at the gala, two well-built men in formal tuxedos rushed forward to open the doors. Susan had told Shelbi in the limo that she would introduce her to a number of people and then, as the gala co-chair, she would be busy for most of the night.

Shelbi held the front of her skirt up as she climbed the red granite stairs. As she looked down at her feet, she thought how spectacular her body art looked in low light.

As they entered the foyer of the building, a number people at the gala turned to Susan and waved at her while others strode toward her. The next 20 minutes were spent introducing Lieutenant Shelbi MacPhadden and Lieutenant Paul Sanders to a variety of people.

Shelbi felt relaxed and started enjoying herself. She knew the night would be a mix of meeting new people and starting relationships, enjoying a wonderful dinner, and dancing with Paul. At the same time, they would be raising donations to help orphan children.

Little did Shelbi know that two completely unexpected major events would unfold at different times that night. One would be very unusual and change the course of her life and save many others. The other would be so personal only she and the other person could ever experience the dynamic and inspiring emotions the unique event would generate forever.

Chapter 4: The Big Gala Event with Surprises and More

A hush rolled across the wide expanse of the gala ballroom that instantly put Shelbi's warrior instincts on edge, as it felt like something tremendous had occurred.

Shelbi hesitated then stopped talking to Keith her sponsor as the hush enveloped them.

"I wonder what is causing this," Shelbi thought as her warrior instincts went on high alert. It was at moments like these she wished she had worn her military uniform with a weapon rather than this magnificent blue evening side split dress she had not been able to hide a weapon under.

Looking back at the entrance, she could see a commotion around a tall elegant lady with flowing golden hair. She was surrounded by a number of people. Everyone in the room who looked her way bowed slightly and seemed to step back to form a human aisle for her to walk through. Moments later, the volume returned to normal hubbub levels.

As Shelbi restarted her conversation with Keith, he stared over her shoulder and seemed to lose focus on what she was saying. Again, her warrior instincts went on full alert as she moved her right foot in front of her left to enable her to move quickly if a defensive move was required. Her right hand grasped her purse, ready to use it as a chopping weapon if needed.

A tall elegant lady wearing a full-length pale yellow dress and a matching pair of short yellow gloves strode up to Shelbi and addressed her.

"You are Lieutenant Shelbi MacPhadden, are you not?" the lady asked.

"Yes, I am Lieutenant Shelbi MacPhadden."

"Good evening. I am First Lady Bitzon, lady to the One Mother," she said and then paused for Shelbi to take in the information. "Lieutenant MacPhadden, the One Mother would like to have a conversation with you, if it's convenient."

Shelbi bowed her head slightly to the young woman. "Good evening, First Lady Bitzon. It is a pleasure to make your acquaintance. Naturally, I would be pleased to have a conversation with the One Mother."

Her defences relaxed when she realized what the situation was and that warmth was projecting from those around her.

As the first lady walked away, Shelbi returned to her conversation with Keith. However, he seemed distracted and finally said, "Shelbi, I don't know if you realize how big an honour it is to have a conversation with the One Mother. It must be about something very special and important. I can leave you now, if you like?" he said with a slight edge of anticipation in his voice.

"Keith, we can keep talking until the One Mother arrives," Shelbi said with a smile.

Moments later, Lady Bitzon arrived followed by the One Mother and a second lady.

First, Lady Bitzon spoke softly, "Lieutenant Shelbi MacPhadden, it is my pleasure to introduce the One Mother."

Shelbi bowed slightly towards the new lady and said, "It is my honour and pleasure to meet you, One Mother."

The One Mother looked Shelbi over from head to toe with a smile on her face. "Very interesting," she said. "It is also my pleasure to have the opportunity to meet you and have a personal conversation with you."

She looked around and turned back to Shelbi saying, "I think it would be better if we went outside on the terrace to speak. Too many people here are already wondering why I'm spending so much time talking to you. Little do they know how important you really are."

Shelbi was somewhat taken aback at the high praise from the One Mother, but slipping into her elite training mode, she graciously accepted the compliment with a slight bow of her head and said, "Thank you for the high honour, One Mother. Yes, I'll be glad to walk with you out on to the terrace."

The two ladies following the One Mother stationed themselves several steps back on the terrace. The One Mother again looked at Shelbi and ran her eyes up and down her toned warrior body.

"You have no idea, do you, Lieutenant MacPhadden? You have no idea about the electric aura and colours surrounding and moving about you?"

"No, One Mother. I do not have the ability to see these electrical colours and auras that you and your people can see around me."

"It is stunning and quite different from the electrical auras around our people," the One Mother remarked.

"One Mother, if you would like to call me Shelbi rather than Lieutenant MacPhadden, I would be honoured."

The One Mother's head tilted back as she laughed heartily. "We are going to be best friends, Shelbi. However, you must always address me as One Mother when we're in public, since that's what people on this planet expect. It's too long a tradition to change."

Shelbi said, "The importance of that for you and your culture is much more important than trying to be casual."

The One Mother then turned to the ladies and asked them to step back a couple of paces. They looked at one another almost as if they had been insulted, then bowed slightly and did as requested.

"I need to talk to you about that moment in time when Phillip changed you and him forever. I'm fully aware of the circumstances and agree wholeheartedly with his assessment and action at the time. As the High Prince, he is sworn to be the protector of all women. However, it was a serious violation of our protocol. He could have been censured or even put in jail," the One Mother said.

Shelbi's warrior control meant her face did not show her concern when she realized what could have occurred because of that one incident. Before her emotions could get any stronger, she thought of what to say next.

The One Mother observed her concern in her electric aura and said, "You should know that I have no way of reading your mind. That joy seems to be only for Phillip. Can you read my thoughts, my dear?"

"Actually, One Mother, I never thought to try."

"Try now, my dear. What am I thinking?"

"I really have no idea. Your thoughts are your own and I have no way of seeing them. The voice in my head when Phillip and I were together has not happened with anyone else."

"Very interesting. However, your electric aura colour changes as you are discussing or saying things. It gives me some understanding of the emotions you are going through. Phillip is my godson, therefore any discussions you have with me are as his godmother and not the One Mother. When he talked about the incident with you and the shift to your mind connections, plus the significant change in your electric aura and colours, I understood. I was quick to make sure that no one else was party to our discussion."

Then she seemed to pause and tilted her head slightly to the right as if thinking. "Shelbi, would you like to see the colours that swirl around our people?"

Shelbi thought for a moment before answering. This would be a unique experience not currently shared by anyone other than the people on this world. "Yes, One Mother, if that were possible, I'd be very interested in seeing the auras that you and your people talk about. It would be a pleasure to be part of such a wonderful opportunity."

It was now the One Mother's turn to look pensive and lost in thought. "We will have to see if we can work that out," she said, almost as if talking to herself. "Oh dear, Shelbi, I better return or there will be all sorts of rumours about what we're doing out here. Ignore any rumours you may hear. It was not my plan to create any problems for you, but people will talk about your private audience with me anyway."

"That will not be a problem, One Mother. I'm used to this kind of thing. People seem to start attributing all sorts of weird and wonderful things to what I can accomplish."

The One Mother nodded and smiled warmly in understanding, then continued, "Shelbi, I would like to have a true private audience with you. I'd like to set up a time when you could come for afternoon tea and we could have a genuine conversation without worrying about people eavesdropping. Would you be agreeable to that?"

It was Shelbi's turn to smile and quickly respond, "Wonderful! I would truly enjoy that and look forward to it.

Let me know when it is convenient for you and I'll make sure I'm available."

The One Mother continued to gaze at Shelbi. As her eyes roamed around her body, she seemed to be thinking. Finally, she spoke up, "Shelbi, could I give you a kiss on the cheek?"

Lady Bitzon had slowly worked her way beside the One Mother. As she heard the One Mother ask that question, she stepped back and gasped.

"Relax, there's nothing ceremonial or significant about this. It's just a friendly god motherly gesture," the One Mother said.

Shelbi was unaware that a kiss from the One Mother was a rare occurrence. She didn't realize the significance until after a horrendous event in the future tied her much closer to the One Mother.

"If you would like to give me a kiss, I would be honoured," Shelbi said.

The One Mother then went a step further, causing both of her ladies' right hands to fly up to their cheeks and gasp in astonishment. The One Mother took off her lace gloves. Handing them to first Lady Bitzon, she reached out and took Shelbi's hands in hers. Looking intently at Shelbi and around her body, it was her turn to gasp. "Absolutely amazing," the One Mother said. She then leaned forward and kissed Shelbi first on the right cheek and then on the left.

As the One Mother firmly grasped Shelbi's hands, she began to feel a warmth spread over her entire body. It made her feel comfortable and eased the tension of dealing with such a high dignitary on this planet. The warmth made her feel equally calm and energized.

She watched as the two ladies took more steps back, and their eyes widened as they looked at Shelbi. She had no idea what was going on but knew that it must have some significance.

"Thank you, Shelbi. This is been very interesting and provided me with many things to think about. And if you could see what just happened to your electric colours, you'd be as astonished as my two ladies."

She let go of Shelbi's hands, replaced her gloves, and smiled at Shelbi before she turned to walk back into the gala room.

The warm glow that surrounded Shelbi seemed to subside. Shelbi decided to wait before going back in since she was unsure how people would react when they saw her glowing aura. Finally, realizing if she stayed up there too long, people would read more significance into that, Shelbi strode back into the room with her long tattooed legs showing with each graceful stride. As she walked into the room, her two close friends, Keith and Susan, were standing by the door. They both bowed slightly.

Finally, Susan spoke excitedly, "Shelbi, an audience with the One Mother. This is absolutely amazing. What did you talk about? No, no, don't tell me. It's probably something private that no one else on the planet is supposed to know about. Can you at least give me a hint?"

Shelbi laughed. "Actually, we just exchanged names and said what a wonderful opportunity it was for me to be here as a representative of the empire."

Susan looked amused. "Really?! You were out on the terrace for all that time and all you had was some idle chitchat!"

"Yes. I'm sure the One Mother does that occasionally at these kinds of affairs," Shelbi said.

"Easy, Shelbi," Keith said. "You have to understand the One Mother rarely, if ever, even attends galas. Too many people want too much from her at these events. In fact, in the 50-year history of this gala, she has never been here before. It is a significant event that she came, and she apparently came specifically to see you."

It was Shelbi's turn to be taken aback. "Susan, Keith, I apologize. I had no idea. Still, I'm not sure she was here just to see me."

Shelbi thought back to when the One Mother stopped before re-entering the gala and said, "Shelbi, I look forward to helping you learn more about our society."

"One Mother, if there's anything I could ever do to repay you, I would be glad to help you in any way possible," Shelbi said.

Little did the One Mother or Shelbi know how significant that one brief sentence would be. When it became a life-and-death situation for the One Mother, Shelbi would become involved and change their worlds forever.

Shelbi slyly smiled, turned to Susan, and said, "Yes, we stopped talking when we decided there was nothing more we could plot. Just kidding!"

Chapter 5: Gala Princely Surprise

Shelbi walked around the charity gala greeting various people. An elegant lady came up to Shelbi and said, "I understand you are wearing a dress designed by Ricardo."

They talked about the dress design and colours. Shelbi learn that the lady had bought a Ricardo dress from one of his early shows. She asked Shelbi about his design process. She smiled when Shelbi talked about walking around nude.

"Maybe I will have him design one for me. When you see him next, tell him Sharon Barrington says hello," she said as she walked away smiling.

She saw an older couple and walked over to them. She had been introduced to Yvonne and Carl Sagamore previously in Susan's house. Carl was a mogul who owned a number of large thriving global businesses. Yvonne, his loving wife of 25 years, had helped start two of his most successful businesses and helped them grow. They were a lovely couple from high society who could be helpful to

Shelbi in both business and socially. Shelbi began talking to them.

Suddenly, Yvonne stepped in front of her husband, scowling. "If that yellow and red electric passion flash you just released is for my husband, young lady, you picked the wrong woman to challenge," Yvonne said with her hands clenched on her hips.

"Passion flash?" Shelbi's eyebrows furrowed in confusion.

"You had a bright yellow and red flare around your body when Carl was talking to you!"

That was when Shelbi realized Prince Phillip had unexpectedly connected and said three words, "Hello, my Shelbi," when she was talking to Carl.

Shelbi started to apologize to Yvonne. "Lady Yvonne, I am truly sorry and I, I am not sure what to say."

The tension was high around them and Shelbi felt she was not doing a good job as Yvonne continued to glare at her.

A deep baritone voice rang out, cutting Shelbi off in the middle of her stammering sentence.

"Uncle Carl and Aunt Yvonne, how good to see you again," Prince Phillip said striding up to them.

Yvonne let out a hardy laugh. She now understood why Shelbi had a passion flare.

"Back from saving the world? Any part of you need reattaching?" Yvonne laughed.

"Ha, ha," Phillip said with a smile. "No, no major parts this time, Aunt Yvonne."

Smiling, Yvonne turned to Shelbi. "I should apologize, my dear. I clearly see now why your electric aura flared. Good for you! Phillip needs a strong woman to corral him!"

"Thanks, Aunt Yvonne, but you should also know Shelbi doesn't see our electric colours. She doesn't really know what you're talking about," Phillip said.

Laughing heartily, Yvonne said, "But, of course, my dear. Oh well, now you both have to come to tea next week."

Yvonne's tea parties were legendary in society and to be invited was almost a command and an honour.

Shelbi thought, "*I can't believe the heat between my inner thighs from seeing my Phillip again. I am getting wet just seeing him standing here.*"

Phillip, clearing his throat, said, "Come outside, Shelbi. We can talk there without attracting too much attention." Phillip thought, "*If I get any harder, everyone will see it. I really want to make love to this beautiful warrior woman!*"

Shelbi heard every thought he had. Her eyes glanced down. She immediately noticed the long shape of his hard manliness pressing against the zipper of his black dress pants.

As they walked outside, Phillip brushed against the top of the slit of Shelbi's amazing dress, just grazing her colourful bare skin. Her stomach flared with passion and warm tingles shot down her legs like liquid heat. The heat set off another wave of wetness between her thighs.

"You're Prince Phillip! Head of the military. Head of agriculture. Heir to the throne. I never knew you were such a powerful person when we were in the academy."

"Yes, and I'm grateful you were one of the few people who liked me as a person rather than those other noble things. They carry so much baggage when people interact with me. It's hard to find out who's a true friend. Women usually just see the power, position, and fortune, not the person behind the titles."

As Shelbi walked ahead, Phillip looked at her long, beautiful, erotic legs gliding in and out of the slit of her blue dress. Her tattoo leg design was so sensual he wanted to reach out and caress every inch of her soft glowing skin. The electric waves flowing around her were so sensual that he got even harder.

He thought back to the moment when he arrived at the gala ball. He had come hoping Shelbi would be there but also out of a sense of duty that he should appear. As one of the patrons of this charity, it was important for him to show up. He had been back on the planet less than two days. As he walked up the steps of the building that housed the gala, he started to greet people. As he entered the room, his eyes gazed across the main room and stopped at a magnificent blue shimmering dress. His eyes ran up the leg with the amazing makeup tattoo. Goodness, he wanted to caress the velvet skin of those legs.

While his manhood started to rise to the occasion and pressed hard against the front of his black dress pants, his eyes swept up to the look at the lady's face. It was Shelbi! His Shelbi! That is when he spoke out in this mind not knowing if she could still hear him.

Shelbi had learned to appreciate him as a warrior. He loved her, but had to keep it hidden as she worked tirelessly to become a Princess Elite and he claimed the right to be a Prince Elite.

Although he fantasised about taking her naked body, caressing it, kissing it, and watching the nipples rise on her bare breasts, he'd never made a move beyond thinking about it in his bedroom late at night.

As true warrior elite professionals, both of them had been very careful to keep their rising erotic emotions for each other hidden. Now he could see Shelbi's electric colours and that rare passion flare in her when she looked at him.

When they graduated, he often thought about finding her, but decided to wait and see what fate had in store for them. If only he truly knew how cruel and unforgiving fate can be.

Shelbi turned to show the magnificent multicoloured tattoo on her leg as her skirt flared.

"Shelbi, do you know what your leg design means?" Phillip asked.

"I was told it would suit me as a warrior princess elite."

"Well, actually, it is the design of the legendary Warrior Princess Shanii who saved our planet," Phillip said.

"I knew it was an interesting design and several people commented on it, but no one told me about the legend. What is it?"

As Phillip began to talk, his fingers traced the swirls on her bare legs. Just his touch on her soft velvet skin made her electric aura swirl around her toned legs, setting off an urge in him to make love to her!

Shelbi was startled at the heat his fingers raised on her ivory skin. The heat started at his fingertips, rolled up her leg across her copper mound, and across her breasts. Her nipples pebbled and vibrated as the heat struck them.

"In our culture, the Second Moon legend says that the warrior princess worked with the Sun God, Euro, to save the planet from being stolen by a rival galaxy's Sun God, Furo. The rival galaxy's sun was burning out and needed to consume the energy from the earth to keep glowing. The warrior princess helped save the planet and the Euro rewarded her with the second moon that gives her light even in the darkness of night. According to the legend, that's why the second moon that follows the first moon is brighter."

Shelbi opened the side of her skirt and looked at the colourful swirls and lines of the tattoo down her right leg.

While Phillip had been talking, his eyes roamed up and down Shelbi's colourful leg. *What an amazing leg. I can't wait to run my lips from that gorgeous ankle up the outside to that incredible curvey hip into that soft skin of her slim waist. Then I'm going to lick her inner leg until I reach her pouting ..."*

"Phillip, I can hear your thoughts, remember!" Shelbi panted. *"I can't wait to feel your lips caressing the inside of my thighs."*

As Phillip watched the fiery electric colours swirl around her fine body, he had more thoughts. *"What I really want is to feel your warm fingers caressing my rock hard manliness."*

Shelbi thought back, *"I can't wait for my hot lips to circle the head of your warm erect manhood."*

Phillip said, "I think I have to leave now, otherwise I'm going to find out what colour that little thong you are wearing is." Then he laughed when he realized he'd said that aloud.

Shelbi reached out and took his hand. *"What thong?"* she thought with a sexy smile on her full red lips.

Phillip watched as her passionate yellow, red, and orange aura flared and simmered around her breasts and curvy hips.

"I want to kiss you on the cheek just once and then I'm going to walk slowly away and command my hardness to deflate!" Phillip thought.

Shelbi twirled around so he could get another good look at her long elegant legs. Her amazing electric colours continued to excite his emotions.

Phillip groaned and thought, *"Shelbi, that is not going to help my manhood settle down."*

"That's the idea," Shelbi thought. "I want you to remember this meeting and these tender moments we've had," she said aloud then she thought, *"And later, my Phillip, you and I are going to spend some passionate time together."*

Phillip leaned forward and kissed the soft skin of her right cheek. *"My God,"* he thought as he drank in the sweet perfume rolling off her neck. *"Her skin is like velvet. She smells like heaven must smell. Her skin is so warm. I just want to keep kissing her!"*

Shelbi tilted her head back and laughed, as if he just whispered some secret joke to her.

"Phillip, I can still hear what you're thinking. Fortunately, this tattoo is waterproof or else it would start to smear between my legs. If I get any wetter, you will have to do something about it and soon."

She knew she couldn't shield her thoughts from this man who would soon be her passionate lover.

Phillip stepped back, eased off his black formal jacket, and folded it over his left arm to hide the bulging front of his dress pants. He smiled and said, "It is wonderful to meet again, Lieutenant MacPhadden."

He slowly began to walk back into the gala. He began to think of a cold shower, but that didn't work. All he thought of was the cold shower turning hot and Shelbi stark-naked with him, leaning back against his bare rippled abs, running his hands over her white shoulders and down her soft side to her thin waist, and then over the velvet skin of her soft curvy hips, his mouth running over her pouting breasts as the warm water trickled off her erect cherry nipples.

"This is not working," Phillip thought as his mind again was linked to Shelbi.

"It's not meant to work, Phillip!" she said with enough passion to keep him on edge, *"but please turn me off and go away."*

They both laughed. There was no way either them was going to be turned off for some time to come.

Shelbi worried about her passion flare and if people could see it as she walked back into the gala. She bumped her funny bone into the edge of a door and hoped the pain would erase the passion flare. However, as she walked back in, several women were smiling and she knew she hadn't been completely successful.

The second last thing she had said to the prince was, "Prince Phillip, I look forward to seeing more of you. Perhaps I could cook lunch for you when your schedule allows."

Phillip looked at her, and thought, *"More of me. I want to see all of you stretched out on a soft, warm blanket lying beside my naked body."* Then out loud for the listeners he commented, "Yes, I will let you know when my schedule is free in the next couple of weeks. Thank you for the invitation. I look forward to talking to you about how we can work together in the agricultural area and learn from your interstellar trade experiences."

Shelbi knew that the words he was speaking were to help her focus and hopefully bring the passion down.

Knowing the prince had just come back from a battle, she said, "Prince Phillip, please take care of your bruises and bangs. *When I see you naked,"* she thought, *"I want you to be all better and I don't want to be distracted by avoiding your deep yellow and blue bruises with my fingers, my lips, my pounding thighs, and anything else of mine I can get on your body."*

Her words had a sense of humour and warm passion. Unfortunately, fate would have a different version of the prince's naked body for Shelbi to stare at as he lay unconscious in his med pod.

Chapter 6: Discovering the Electric Body Flow

Shelbi did not know about the enormous consequences this casual meeting with the One Mother would have on her life, the One Mother's life, Prince Phillip's life, and many others. Catastrophic events would unfold that, combined with a dynamic and emotionally charged enemy, would write a page in history for this planet.

Shelbi neared the massive sculptured gates of the One Mother's estate and slowly turned up the long gravel driveway. She was amazed that the nano chip in her shoulder allowed the gates to unlock. Yesterday, when the One Mother's tech person had placed a tiny dot on her shoulder, she wondered how they could know what the code would be since it was changed randomly every day.

"Technology is wonderful", she thought, *"especially when it works."*

Before she reached the top of the brown stone porch steps, the front door opened and a magnificent tall, broad-shouldered man with silver hair and a big smile stood in the doorway.

"Welcome, Lieutenant Shelbi," he said with a rich baritone voice.

Shelbi knew this was the One Mother's husband, Earl Hargett Stone. She had been briefed on the personal side of the One Mother's life, which is often kept from the public's knowledge. The man who stood before her had given up his command in the military and chose to stay by the One Mother's side because he loved her so deeply. His children would never carry his name, and one of his daughters would take over as the One Mother one day.

Lady Bitzon had given Shelbi some background on how the young, dashing military hero had met the One Mother when she was still a lady and had yet to reach her pinnacle position. He had met her at the Gonfor Charity Gala and fell hopelessly in love with her. At first, she rejected him knowing that her life would be entirely different as the

One Mother. Yet, she knew she would marry and hoped to find a man she loved.

When she first met him, she felt that he was arrogant. He walked tall and with purpose towards her. He introduced himself with a flare and a low bow. Rather dramatic. Rather theatrical. And she thought him rather overblown. However, when he reached out to take her hand and gently kissed the back of it, an electric yellow charge went through her body that she could not have anticipated. He noticed the change and smiled warmly.

"My name is Earl Hargett Stone and I would like the pleasure of this dance," he said with a sensual note that only a man who was falling in love could bring to a conversation.

She smiled and said, "Yes, I would like to dance."

This short conversation changed their destiny for good. As they danced, they both felt so comfortable with each other that it seemed they had known each other for a long time. By the end of the dance, their fate was sealed.

People generally don't believe in love at first sight. They're wrong. Some of the strongest loves ever sow their seed when they first meet.

Shelbi reached the door and put out her hand, which Earl shook warmly. "Please come into our house," he said with a smile.

From the outside, it looked like a small bungalow, but as she entered, she began to realize that the property extended back a long way.

As Earl turned, he said, "I have the pleasure of escorting you to the One Mother."

Earl walked with Shelbi into a beautiful living room where the One Mother was seated in a chair with two people either side of her. They were laughing and having an interesting conversation that stopped as soon as Shelbi entered the room. The One Mother immediately rose and walked quickly to her.

"Shelbi, it's a great delight to have you here. Hopefully, today you will learn a little bit more about your electric body flow. I hope you enjoy it and do not find it too shocking."

It was Shelbi's turn to laugh. "One Mother, it's always interesting to learn new things. I look forward to it."

The One Mother turned and introduced the two people with her. "Shelbi, this is Dr. Uxbridge. He's here to help you manage your reaction. This is Dr. Swanson, or Specs, as we like to call her. She's been working on the technology and design of the lenses we want to share with you today that will allow you to see your body's electric aura."

Shelbi reached out. "Dr. Uxbridge, it is my pleasure to meet you. I hope I don't tax you too much today. Dr. Swanson, thank you very much for your help with this interesting opportunity."

Dr. Swanson was a taller version of Shelbi. Her hips were broad, her breasts full, and her lips 'eager for kissing.'

"Today I'm going to unlock more than just your ability to see the electric flow. You'll be able to feel the emotions and understand things like you never have before. Not just as a warrior, but as the spectacular woman your shape tells me you are. After today, when you wear the lenses while making love, it will be an emotionally erotic feeling that you can't imagine right now," Dr. Swanson said with warmth.

Shelbi was slightly shocked by how frank and forward Dr. Swanson was, but she had been warned by the One Mother that before she moved forward, she had to think about the unintentional consequences of what was about to happen.

"Once we unlock your ability to see the emotional electric flare around your body, it will change your perception of the person you are with. The erotic nature when making love can be overwhelming for people who've not been trained to manage it," the One Mother told her. "I want to make sure you understand this will change your perception of the people around you significantly."

Dr. Swanson picked up what looked like an eyeglass case and handed it to the One Mother. The One Mother sat down on the couch and invited Shelbi to sit with her.

"Shelbi, here are the golden lenses that you can slip on like any contact lens. These ones will last for about three minutes before they evaporate into the atmosphere. Dr. Swanson has worked with your Special Program Elite Intelligence Management technology machine to understand your metabolism and other physical factors typical of your species. When you first see the colours, it will be overwhelming. Don't be embarrassed if you have an erotic reaction from finally seeing something that is so new, so different, and so wonderful," the One Mother said.

Shelbi hadn't really thought about there being an audience when she was doing this. She hadn't thought about the fact that her nipples might get hard in front of these people, especially the One Mother!

"I understand what you're saying, One Mother, but I won't really know until I try it."

The One Mother handed Shelbi the round red and blue case and told her to put the golden lenses on her eyes and then close them quickly.

"I will tell you when to open your eyes, Shelbi. Both Dr. Swanson and Dr. Uxbridge will be here to understand what's going on and to take readings to see how to improve the technology for you."

Shelbi carefully inserted the soft golden contact lenses and quickly closed her eyelids. The slight warmth spread across her eyes and she realized the nano technology was working.

"Shelbi, open your eyes now," the One Mother said.

Shelbi opened her crystal blue eyes and looked around. She flinched. Everyone in the room had distinctive electric aura colours of oranges, yellows, and reds rolling around their bodies. Each one was so beautiful, so wonderful, it brought tears to the corners of her eyes.

Dr. Swanson spoke softly to Shelbi, "How do they feel?"

Shelbi said, with a slight catch in her throat, "They're amazing. They feel warm, and I can see all these amazing yellow, reds, and orange colours flowing around your bodies. It's absolutely spectacular!"

Dr. Uxbridge then asked her, "How do they fit and how do they feel on your eyeballs."

"They feel great! They are slightly warm but not uncomfortable at all."

The One Mother rose and spoke to Shelbi, "I want to show you a little of what you can expect in the lovemaking area."

Shelbi's eyes opened wider with uncertainty. Earl walked over and gave his wife a gentle hug and a full kiss. Shelbi watched as the colours around them swirled and overlapped as he kissed her. The red electric lines seemed to flow and sparkle. The One Mother stepped back and laughed. Shelbi saw the colours swirl again in different patterns.

"Shelbi, the lenses will start to evaporate in a moment. We have three more sets for you. Each set will last a little longer than the previous one, just so you can get used to wearing them," she said. "What you really need to do is go home, get naked, and watch your own electric colours change in response to your touch."

Shelbi could see her colours changing and swirling as the One Mother talked about her getting naked. She could feel her nipples puckering at the thought of how erotic it might look. She felt a simmering heat between the vee in her legs. She physically shook her head. These were not the thoughts she should be having around people who could see how her colours were reacting.

No one said a word. They knew part of what she was going through because they had all been there before themselves. They realized how overwhelming it was for Shelbi to see for the first time something they all enjoyed in their lovemaking so tremendously.

Back in her house, in her own private bedroom, Shelbi stripped and hung up her clothes. Holding the next set of lenses, she looked down at her naked body and wondered how it would feel and how the electric colours would flow over her soft skin as she began to masturbate.

She slipped the lenses into her eyes. She lay down on her soft white bed covers. When she opened her eyes, she saw reds, yellows, and oranges swirling around her body. As she cupped her ample breasts, it looked as if the orange was spurting from her nipples and then rolling across and up her breasts towards her shoulders. The red around her shoulders collided with the rolling orange and created beautifully sensuous patterns.

"Oh my God, this is really one of the most beautiful and sensual things I have ever seen."

Her hands fluttered down her stomach towards her copper mound and she brushed her fingers through the short hair. The colours exploded with oranges and reds, making it almost seem as if she was on fire! She knew the electric colours didn't actually generate heat, but it certainly felt like it. The wave of heat rolled down between the vee of legs and she began to feel moist.

The reds and yellows on the inside of her thighs began to swirl as she ran her fingers lightly above her inner milky thighs. Her vagina lips were moist and starting to pout. She wanted to touch them, to caress them, but was still too eager to see how the colours rolled around before actually engaging her fingers with her hot flesh.

She squeezed her bare breasts together. The colours exploded and swirled around each breast, twirled around each of her rose-coloured erect nipples, and then rolled around her hands as they held her warm breasts.

She was beginning to pant. Then she noticed something she hadn't seen in anyone else's colours. A thin purple strand seemed to roll up from between her thighs, over her stomach, and swirled around her breasts, finally plunging off her tented nipples.

"No one ever mentioned a purple electrical line. I wonder what that means."

Her aching vagina lips could wait no longer. As she moved her right hand down and started to caress herself, the reds and oranges swirled around and up her fingers and across her wet vagina lips. The strand of purple also joined and shot up her stomach as the warmth expanded.

She moved her fingers up and down her moist full lips between her thighs. Shelbi began to understand how she wanted to play with her erect clitoris. She noticed that an amazing red and orange electric light was dancing around it, making it feel hot and sensuous just with the mere sight of those electric waves.

Her hand plucked the tingling nipple on her left breast and she saw the electric colours explode and roll around her fingers as the warm sensation enveloped her nipple and made it even harder.

She wanted to close her eyes as she stroked herself and began to build towards a climax, but could not because of the amazing colours rolling around her creamy skin.

Her fingers slowly felt down to her throbbing clitoris and pouting lips. Using her thumb and her forefinger, she began to caress the swollen bud. Again, colours burst and swirled all around her body as she rubbed the tender nub harder and harder and harder.

She ran her left palm over her right nipple and saw the electric yellows and reds swirl and explode. Then her fingers moved over to her left nipple and more reds and oranges exploded. As her climax was building, she noticed the purple rolling up her stomach, around her breasts, and back down again.

She took her fingers away, began to lick them, and watched the electric colours exploding around her pink wet fingers and off her full red lips.

Shelbi realized the colours were starting to fade as the lenses began to evaporate. She continued to work her sensitive, erect clitoris and finally slipped two fingers inside her dripping vagina.

Finally, she could wait no longer. Her nipples were so hard they ached as she plucked at them with her left finger.

She stroked her southern lips, plunging her fingers inside, and rubbing her clitoris with her thumb. She continued to work towards her climax.

As Shelbi could feel it coming, she opened her eyes. She felt her climax flutter across her legs and thighs and could still see the colours exploding around her. The purple was amazing and seemed to tingle as it touched her white skin. Her hips bucked and legs clenched together as one of the most amazing climaxes she had ever had alone rocked her vibrating body. The wetness between her thighs seemed to be on fire and sensual at the same time.

She lay back with a slight sheen of perspiration on her naked body. She opened her eyes and could no longer see the colours. She had to wait 24 hours before putting in the next set of lenses and could hardly wait. She thought of the colours that must roam around Phillip's body.

As she drifted off to sleep, she thought, *"I wonder what colour his erect throbbing manhood throws off just before it enters my hot wet vagina."*

Chapter 7: Charting New Virgin Territory

Shelbi ran her warm hands down the soft sides of her bare body. Her right fingertips fluttered across her creamy compact stomach and stopped at her trimmed copper mound. She tugged her short curly red hair back and forth then she stepped into the warm water of her shower. She began to think of the events that led to this fun-filled day.

After the gala, she and Phillip had met occasionally at business meetings. They had tried to have coffee together several times, but never managed to connect due to business commitments. Finally, she sent him a message: *Phillip, it's time to charter new territory.*

Since the days at the warrior academy, this had been one of their ongoing moments of humour. Very early on, he said that charting virgin territory was always fun as long as both parties were able to map it together.

As part of her message, she had said, *"Let's meet at 3 o'clock in my field office."* He responded quickly: *"Yes, let's start charting at 3 o'clock. There's a lot of virgin territory to be mapped."*

Phillip walked out of his exercise room, stripping off his damp t-shirt. Rotating his shoulders and feeling the muscles ripple across his back, he knew it had been a light workout to get him ready for his exercise with Shelbi. He stepped into the shower and washed in the lightly scented custom-made shower gel that Shelbi had reacted positively to before. She had said, "That's the manliest, most wonderful scent I have ever smelled! It is very erotic."

As Shelbi continued to soap her body, she thought back to the early morning trip to her spaceship for routine checks. She had also checked her lab results on the computer and found that her med lab had developed the right formula to coat her vagina. Shelbi had learned to protect herself on other alien worlds from diseases and pregnancy. It would not be wise to conceive the prince's child on this world.

She lay naked on the table while the lights were lowered and the stirrups adjusted to spread her long legs. The warm insertion device sprayed a sweet-smelling coating on her vagina lips then it slowly continued sliding in and continued to spray protective coating on the sensitive walls of her canal. This process always made her feel warm and erotic.

"Perhaps you should only do it once," she said to the med computer.

The computer answered, "We need to make sure it works effectively. You'll have to endure three more applications."

Shelbi placed her hands on the tops of her bare breasts, determined not to arouse herself any more than necessary. By the time she got to the fourth and final spray insertion, she was close to having an orgasm.

***

The prince continued to lather his broad shoulders and stretched the muscles once more in the hot water. He wanted to make sure he was ready to explore virgin territory.

His mind drifted back to the first time he saw Shelbi naked. They had been out on patrol with several other warriors. The facility in the camp only had one shower for non-commissioned men and women. He had looked to see the green flag on the door to make sure it was free. He opened it and then stopped short as his eyes took in a naked female bending over with her back to him. As she stood up and turned around, he glanced at a fully nude Shelbi MacPhadden. She stood still as his eyes roamed down her body, across her broad naked curvy hips, and focused on her amazing copper mound.

"My gosh, that is amazing. So sensual!" he thought. No one in his world had red hair and he found it amazing, erotic, and unusual.

"Don't you knock before you enter a room?" Shelbi accused.

"See the green flag here, Private Shelbi! You forgot to turn it to red and lock the door."

She laughed and turned away from him. He turned the green to red and walked out knowing the door would lock behind him.

Phillip continued to lather his legs and abdomen and thought about Shelbi naked. His manhood was starting to get hard.

"I wonder if I'm going to be too big for her," he thought. *"I'll have to make sure I go slowly. I would never want to hurt her."*

***

Shelbi emerged from the bathroom and applied some makeup. She slid her white lacy bikini underpants up her legs and felt the warmth in the vee of between her naked thighs. She put on the matching white lace bra. Next was her sunflower yellow linen pants, and last, a matching linen tunic that dropped over her board womanly hips.

***

Phillip emerged from his bathroom and decided to go commando for the day. He put on a pair of charcoal grey pants that accented his backside but weren't too tight in the front. He put on a dark blue short-sleeved shirt so his muscular arms could move freely.

***

Shelbi got the security cam notice that Phillip had entered the front gates. She opened the doors as he walked up the steps and a smile broke across his lips.

"Wow, you look stunning in yellow with your red hair!" Phillip exclaimed.

"You're not too shabby yourself, Phillip. Are you ready to chart some virgin territory?" she smiled seductively.

"You know I love to charter virgin territory, but I'd really like to have a look at this house first. I'm not sure if you know but it was one of the first cottages developed by the architect Daniel Prello. It's interesting because Susan and

Keith were patrons of his education and he actually built this as part of his graduation project. It's historic, as cottages go on our world."

Shelbi smiled. "I'd love to show it to you. It has an amazing feeling. It's almost as if the house wraps itself around you and makes you feel welcome."

They walked down a short hall that emerged into the wonderfully yellow living and dining room combined. The end of the dining room had a pair of white wooden doors that opened out on to a wonderful landscape garden. Just at the edge, the oval swimming pool could be seen.

After spending some time looking at the house and actually talking about the architect and how he had developed the design, Shelbi asked Phillip if he would like some wine.

"Yes, wonderful," Phillip said.

Shelbi had introduced Phillip to an Earth wine called Merlot. He had immediately loved the rich taste and unique flavours.

Shelbi took out a bottle and pulled out the cork. Pouring it into the glass, she accidentally hit the edge the glass and spilled red wine on to the counter and her yellow pants. She immediately stripped off the pants saying, "I need to soak these immediately or the wine will destroy them."

"Absolutely. This is an interesting start to virgin chartering."

Phillip could feel his manhood hardening as he looked at her bare shapely legs. He began to think of what was hidden under the rest of her clothing. "You have such amazing legs, my Shelbi," he said with a husky voice.

Shelbi walked over, took his hand, and said, "We didn't look at the master bedroom, did we! Come this way and I'll show you the architect's interesting design."

Taking Phillip by the hand, they walked down a short redwood panelled hall to two doors with spectacular glass mosaic designs looking out on the beautiful lush landscape garden. A large king-size bed was centred against one of the walls.

Shelbi walked over to the double door while Phillip stood just inside the bedroom. Knowing that the sunlight would shine across her body and sparkle in her red hair, she turned to Phillip and said, "It's a wonderful view to wake up to in the morning. Since it faces east, the light flows across it as the sun comes up."

Phillip looked at Shelbi and said, "I think it's time to view some virgin territory." A thickness entered his voice as he finished the sentence.

As they started undoing buttons, their excitement rose. Shelbi could see Phillip's manhood getting harder and harder in his pants. Warmth spread down her breasts to between her legs. She could feel her wetness building in anticipation. Shelbi slowly took off her linen tunic to reveal the lacy white bra and white bikini underwear. She then turned back to Phillip as the sunlight created a sensual glow around her. Phillip took his shirt off to reveal his hard chest muscles.

Shelbi looked at Phillip and said, "I think it's time to uncover more territory," as she reached up behind and undid her bra. Her left arm held the bra from falling off her breasts as her right hand moved the bra straps off her bare shoulders.

Phillip's erection was strong and hard at the front of his pants. He was focused on her creamy breasts. Her pink nipples had hardened and were aching. She knew she was getting even moister between her thighs as she turned and dropped the bra on the chair behind her. Phillip crossed the room in three strides and kissed her full on her pouting lips.

Her pert aching nipples pressed against his toned stomach. She could feel his erect manhood press hot and hard against her bare stomach and she knew she was wet and ready for him to stroke her pulsating vagina lips.

He tenderly caressed her cheeks with the back of his warm fingers. Then he leaned in and placed butterfly kisses on her neck as her warm fingertips rubbed across his tanned muscular back.

"His back feels so warm, so manly. I can't wait to be on top of him and kiss his strong arms," Shelbi thought.

Suddenly he tensed. He stepped back and dropped to one knee, holding his head in his hands, exclaiming with real agony, "No, no, no!"

When he looked up and their eyes met, Shelbi immediately shifted from erotic half-naked nymph to warrior stance. The agony in his eyes was clear as his body tensed completely.

"The Sergoymils have kidnapped the One Mother!" Phillip cried out.

She reached out her hand and touched his naked shoulder. "Go, Phillip. Go now!"

Phillip stood and took one last look at her half-naked body, but didn't really see it. He dressed and walked quickly out.

Shelbi's mind was racing. She followed him and exclaimed, "Project Beta."

Phillip turned and looked at her, "Thank you. Yes, initiate a Project Beta," he said with pain in his voice.

Shelbi shut the front door, walked quickly back to her bedroom, and dressed. She then moved to her home office upstairs, opened her computer, and started working on Project OMP Save.

She knew that Phillip was the protector of all women on this planet. He would have plans in place to rescue the One Mother, but her warrior princess elite training kicked in. There should always be a backup plan, a Project Beta.

She began to explore various scenarios, just as her elite training had prepared her for. Shelbi hoped Phillip would stay safe as he rescued the One Mother. She focused on her task. What should she be considering? Where would this rescue be executed? That and many more questions raced through her head and into the computer.

Little did she know that her Project One Mother Prince Beta would be needed if the One Mother and Prince Phillip were ever to be seen alive again.

Chapter 8: A Rescue Gone Wrong

With his heart racing and adrenaline pumping through his body, Phillip ran towards his car, activating it with his grey fob even before he reached it. He yanked the door open, jumped in, and thumbed the auto touchscreen awake. He keyed in the code only known by three people for Operation Phoenix.

Based on the legend bird from Earth, they had named the project Phoenix to rescue the One Mother should she ever be kidnapped. They would rise from the ashes and fire that action created. It automatically linked him to his second in command, John North.

"John, status!" Phillip yelled.

"Yes, the One Mother has been abducted by the Sergoymils. They invaded her private home killing several of the patrol guards outside. They then gassed the people in the house. They only took the One Mother and made their escape."

"Do we have any other information?" Phillip asked.

"We actually have quite a bit. One of the Sergoymils rogues had a faulty nose filter. When they let the gas out in the house, he was overcome, and fell down the spiral stairs breaking a leg and arm. There's some sort of gel in the suit that encased the broken limbs. The Sergoymils didn't take him. They did stab him with a poisoned needle, but they stuck it in the gel and the gel absorbed it, so he was alive but unconscious when our medics got there."

"Was he given that truth-inducing needle? Has he told us anything?" Phillip asked.

"Yes. We know there was one starfighter specially equipped to take three people. The One Mother was taken in that. The others also jumped in starfighters and took off. We know that the One Mother was taken to a small medical ship that is being taken to a quiet destination to interrogator her. They know the political firestorm that will happen, so they want to keep where she's hidden quiet so we can't rescue her."

"I'll be there in nine minutes. We can start confirming which strategy in the plan to activate. Get our Project Phoenix team starfighters ready to go."

Phillip's mind began to race. If they had taken her to a small medical vessel, there is every chance they could find it, overwhelm them, and rescue the One Mother.

He arrived at the strategic central building and slid his car to a screeching halt in a parking spot outside the front door. As he ran up the stairs, an armed guard opened the frosted glass doors. Without breaking stride, he ran through and turned left down the short green corridor.

When he entered the strategic room, he learned they had gleaned more information from the captured Sergoymils. They knew that once the enemy starfighters delivered the One Mother to the medical ship, they were going to jump back through hyperspace into the mainstream. This way the

Sergoymils' government could stall and pretend they don't know what is going on because all their starfighters would be accounted for in their battle zones or home bases.

John confirmed what Phillip had thought on the drive over. Sergoymils used medical ships for interrogation. Medical ships could not be military targets under the Universal Galaxies Treaty. They did not carry arms but were shielded to protect them from stray missiles in a war zone. They were often kept out of the war zone at secret locations. This reduced the chance for accidents from stray missiles, lasers, or gunfire.

This also meant that Phillip could not take big warrior ships to attack the medical ship or they would be in violation of the Universal Galaxies Treaty. He knew that the Sergoymils would have just shot several of their own and put them in med pods to prove their position that they were an active med ship supporting some war effort. This meant that Phillip would only be able to take starfighters without missiles.

John had also learned from their prisoner where the medical interrogation ship was hiding. It was definitely in a different galaxy that most people avoided. It was in a highly unstable area that had experienced a super nova 50,000 years before, leaving debris and shattered planets floating in space.

The three starfighters took off having established their final plan. The prince would gain entry to the medical interrogation vessel under the guise of a ship in distress carrying a pilot with potential injuries. As a medical vessel, they could not refuse a distress call. Once he was on the ship, he would gain control of it and rescue the One Mother.

They dropped out of hyperspace and immediately cloaked all three ships.

The medical ship was exactly where they anticipated. It was a typical Sergoymils medical ship with no armaments or missiles.

A heat scan noted they were 14 people on board. One of them would be an interrogator, another would be the One Mother, one would be the captain, and the remainder medical crew and purposely wounded military personnel. No active military personnel or big weapons were noted. A quick scan of the area showed no other enemy ships in the area.

Phillip uncloaked his ship and activated the program that would make it appear as if his ship was in distress. The distress code went out and the Sergoymils medical officer answered.

"Starfighter, this is medical ship 991133. Identify your problem."

"Starfighter 166836 here. I believe I have thermo drive malfunction. Damage caused by impact outside the hyper wave of particles striking the starboard side. I may have some radiation skin damage. I am also losing oxygen," Phillip said.

"Please seal your weapons. Approach slowly, if possible."

"Weapons locked down. Only small thrusters available. I'll be careful as I approach."

Phillip nudged the ship closer. He then asked permission to come aboard after suiting up since he was losing oxygen in his ship and didn't have a connection to lock in to their airlock hatches.

He was granted permission and went towards the airlock that they designated for his arrival. After entering, the airlock's outer door closed, and he took off his helmet and gloves. The inner door opened. The captain came toward him with his hand out.

"Welcome, captain. Let's get you to the medical area to see about those potential radiation burns."

Phillip realized his error as his arm automatically came up and he shook the captain's hand. He was momentarily distracted and did not notice the young Sergoymils nurse behind him. The next thing he felt was the tranquilizing needle prick his neck and he collapsed out cold on the floor. Right then, John yelled into his earpiece and the words came out loud enough for captain and nurse to hear. The captain started to sneer.

Scramble. Trap. Scramble.

As Phillip fell on the deck, five enemy military ships uncloaked. One was a super dreadnought capable of taking the medical ship inside its cargo hole. The others were two dreadnoughts and the two super starfighters with enough fire power to take out several major empire ships.

The two cloaked starfighters that had come with Phillip knew they were outgunned and immediately uncloaked and jumped in hyperspace. They released a drone to inform others their prince was captured given the firepower of the surrounding ships. Now they had to develop a plan to save both the One Mother and Phillip.

The Sergoymils captain laughed and looked at his two prisoners. The One Mother and Prince Phillip would be taken to the Sergoymils high security war criminals prison. No one had ever escaped it. The captain was confident that until the politicians negotiated the release of a significant number of captured Sergoymils prisoners, the One Mother and the prince would be staying with them.

The two starfighters arrived back at Cirtece. They reported their complete mission failure to command and the capture of the prince.

Shelbi had been in contact with the command team just after Phillip left. She had shared the One Mother Prince Beta plan that was developed by her elite warrior strategic team on her home base.

It was a high-risk plan but Shelbi felt confident that she and others from her elite warrior team could pull it off. Given the importance of the One Mother to the galaxy and the prince to this world, the warrior elite team had worked overtime to devise a plan to ensure they would be returned to their rightful place if Phillip's plan failed.

Project One Mother Prince beta was activated 28 minutes after the warriors returned with their bleak report. Shelbi communicated with her warrior elite strategic group.

Immediately a number of warrior elite princesses and princes began to activate their plan roles for the rescue attempt.

If it worked, they would save the One Mother and Phillip with the added bonus of shaming the Sergoymils. If it failed, Shelbi MacPhadden and many others would die.

Chapter 9: The Big Escape (Almost)

Warrior alert, blood pounding, Shelbi approached the green prison corridor and turned with the lunch wagon she was pushing towards the two Sergoymils warriors guarding Prince Phillip.

The brown shift dress she wore hugged her narrow waist and flared over her hips, barely covering her bare white ass. The silver metallic vagina ring hung down between her thighs for all to see. She placed the meal in front of the first guard who barely looked at her and replied with a curt, "Thank you."

She uncovered the second guard's lunch and placed it down. His hand shot out between her thighs, grabbing the ring and pushing his finger against her cold, dry vagina lips.

She peed, gushing yellow urine on his dark brown hand. He yelled, leapt out of his seat, and backhanded her across the head, sending her sprawling on the floor, legs apart with her black hairy crotch for all to see.

Then he let out a guttural laugh. "You little monkey. You like to play dirty. I see that. We'll have some fun later."

Turning to his companion, he said in his native language, "I'm going to clean this girl's stink off my hands."

As he strode away, Shelbi got up and said, "I will get a rag and some disinfectant and clean this up."

Shelbi came back from the waste closet with a blue terry cloth and a sliver spray can. She got down on her hands and knees with her butt towards the guard so he could see her bare ass, scar-covered legs, and the glinting vagina rang.

"No need to show me your treasures, little one," the guard said softly. Then in his native language, which he didn't know Shelbi understood, he said, "I don't know why they humiliate these people. They're going to rise up some day and get even with us for defiling their women."

Shelbi started by cleaning farther away from the guard's desk. The other guard came back, ruffled Shelbi's hair, laughed, and said, "You little monkey. I can't wait to swing you on my big branch!"

Shelbi moved closer and sprayed the urine splotches on the floor. The mist rose up thinly in the air and the two guards sucked it in. It stunned them. Three seconds later, she jumped to her feet. She clapped her hands twice and turned as four of her team strode into the corridor and up to the guards.

The first pair quickly picked up the first stunned guard and put his handprint and eyes to the security pad on the prince's cell. The second pair took the other stunned guard and used his eyes and hands to open the cell.

Shelbi pulled off the brown rough shift and stood naked for all to see. The other warrior princesses and princes ignored her nakedness since this was a mission, not pleasure time.

Shelbi's prosthetics were working perfectly to disguise her as Jackie Zogdno, a native of the planet. One warrior princess, who knew it was a disguise, also knew it was modelled on a real woman. She briefly noted her yellow arm bruises, the deformed left breast, and the scar inside her left leg. *"I wonder what happened to this little one,"* she thought.

Her fingers dug into the top of the scar on her thigh pulling out two stem patches as she strode through the open door and over to the bed the prince lay on. She gasped when she saw the extent of the bruises covering his body. In one swift motion, she clapped her left hand on the side of his neck.

His eyes jerked open as he sucked in air. She linked her mind to him and said one word, *"Domino."* It immediately relaxed the prince, as it was the command safe word to link two people together in battle.

Her right hand slid up his leg. As the back of her hand touched his limp manhood, she jammed her hand against his bare inner thigh, driving the second stem patch into his skin.

She stepped back as the prince started to sit up. Placing her hand on his bare shoulders, she said, "Wait, wait just a moment, Prince Phillip."

She reached into the second scar on her left leg, pulling out two small objects that she jammed up each of the prince's nostrils. "Filters," she said, "You're going to need these for this elite operation."

Another warrior princess had entered the cell. She handed Shelbi an orange top and skirt then moved to the prince and helped him into an orange jumpsuit. Shelbi grabbed the prince's hand and dragged him outside.

A huge Sergoymils centurion supervisor with a silver metallic helmet, black face shield, and a large wand approached them. The prince linked with Shelbi's mind and said, *"Peace."*

The centurion whipped out the wand, touching the prince's right sleeve, and changed the orange jumpsuit to grey. In one swift motion, he turned and touched Shelbi's right sleeve and her top turned grey, while her skirt turned black. The only words he spoke were, "My prince!"

Shelbi and the prince quickly emerged from the green corridor, picked up the two tech boxes on the floor, and moved away.

The enemy with their over-puffed egos had designed the prison so that maximum security prisoners were held together. In the next green corridor would be the One Mother's cell.

As they walked around the corner, two guards strode towards them. At first, they seemed to ignore them, but as they got closer, one leered at Shelbi.

"Well, little one, do you have two rings I can tug on?" he sneered.

His hand reached out, grabbed Shelbi between the thighs, and found the vagina ring to jerk on. Shelbi's reflexes overrode her thinking as her elbow snapped his nose, sending red blood spurting. As he reeled back and started to pull his weapon out, Phillip knelt down and swept him off his feet, banging the guard's head on the floor. The other guard was stunned for a moment and then began to react, but not fast enough. Shelbi chopped him in the throat and drove her left hand into his stomach.

As they moved into fighter stance, two people entered the hall and quickly got behind the guards and sprayed their faces, knocking them unconscious.

"Thank God for my nose filters," the prince thought.

The two unconscious guards were stuffed into a nearby waste closet. As the prince stared at Shelbi, a thought ran through his groggy head. *"When she was naked in front of them in the cell, she had a black hairy crotch. Wasn't hers red?"* Then the thought was gone as the mission overtook him.

As Shelbi and Phillip rounded the corner, three sets of warrior princesses and princes were standing near the three stunned Sergoymils guards. The guards were quickly whipped up in front of the cell holding the One Mother for the handprint and retina scan.

By the time Shelbi and Phillip reached the door, it was open. Again, Shelbi tapped opened the scar area on her left leg and pulled out two stem patches. They were shocked when they saw the extent of the bruises covering the One Mother's body as she lay naked and fragile on the bed.

Shelbi strode quickly over beside her, jamming her left hand to her neck. Her hand worked up the inside of her bruised thighs and jammed a second stem pad into her thigh.

The prince linked to the One Mother by placing his hand on her shoulder. "Don't move, my One Mother. We are here to save you," he whispered.

He helped her upright in the bed. A warrior princess quickly entered the cell with an orange jumpsuit and helped the One Mother into it. She stood up shakily but knew she had to keep moving. The three emerged from the cell and once again were startled by a large centurion. In one movement, he touched the One Mother's right sleeve and it turned light purple on the top and dark purple on the bottom. Quickly he moved and did the same to the prince and Shelbi. They were now Sergoymils prison electronic workers.

They rounded the corner, picked up their electronic kits, and started to walk. A shrill alarm sounded. Shelbi worried they had been discovered, but kept walking, forcing Phillip and the One Mother to do the same. The lights dimmed in all the hallways as an announcement came over the speakers.

"Fire, fire in quadrant four. Evacuation of quadrant four now in progress."

"Good, right on time," Shelbi thought. *"We are on the other side of the prison in quadrant one."*

Doors to courts and halls started to slam shut as the cells and guards were isolated. Shelbi, Phillip, and the One Mother moved to the nearest escalator and took it down to the meeting area. They moved into the corridor towards the lockers were all the workers were going for routine fire evacuation. Two people came up and separated the One Mother and Phillip, taking them in different directions.

Shelbi went into a closet and took off her clothing disguise. As planned, the brown shift with her identity code had been transferred there by a member of the warrior elite team. She put on the shift and walked past the electronic security scanner and guard booth into the communal change room.

She stripped off her brown shift and stood naked amongst the hundreds of other men and women in similar state. Another sign of the enemy's forced humiliation. She pushed the ring between her vaginal lips in to stop it swinging and so no one could grab it.

She slid away, took an orange jumpsuit out of a locker, and put it on. All the workers who left the building wore the bright orange jumpsuits with large black crosses on the back. They were the property of the enemy. They didn't have their names on their jumpsuits, merely ID numbers sewn into them. A face scan when they left or they entered set up their pay and their security trace in the prison.

Shelbi went out to the parking lot and got into a car with four other people. The car left the parking lot with everyone laughing and apparently distracted.

Shelbi was worried. This was the part of the plan she was the most concerned about. They were now separated and were due to meet up at her spaceship at the same time. If they didn't, they would be left behind.

Shelbi's route was the longest so she would arrive last. This was the plan so any unusual movement around her spaceship would not be noticed. If it was, anyone would think it was maintenance, as she as the owner of the ship was not there.

She finally arrived at her spaceship. As she crossed the black, hot tarmac, someone walked by and said the mission code word that everything was still on plan: "Nazemma." She breathed a small sigh of relief.

She moved into the ship and a warrior princess smiled and handed her personal suit, patted her on the shoulder, and left without saying a word. Shelbi pulled off the jumpsuit and pulled on her white skin suite and the compression suit then locked the helmet in place.

Knowing that her passengers were safely loaded, she jumped into her command chair. Her fingers danced over the controls and sent a link to the tower. The nose filters were irritating her. The vagina ring she had tucked inside her sore vagina would be sensuous at any other time, but now it was just damned scratchy and annoying.

She was slightly early but had time to prepare to leave with the 147 ships that were launching in one caravan for protection during the evacuation. They would go to the gate for hyperspace and 10 to 12 ships would be launched at a time.

Tension rose as the tower communicated she would be delayed due to a technical error, but this was quickly resolved. As a private med-ship plus the right bribe to the tower dispatcher, she was given approval to leave. She joined the other ships in the caravan and moved towards the jump gate.

Several communications were heard about problems at the prison. She wondered if they had discovered that the One Mother and the prince were gone. Then she was at the gate and jumped. She been awake for over 26 hours and was near exhaustion. She didn't dare use another stem patch to keep going. Three was the maximum recommended dose for one day and she had already used four. She set the ship on automatic and wearily rose from her command chair.

She slipped off the helmet and suit. She put the suit back on the rack and connected the chargers. Then she peeled off her white sweat-soaked skin suit and put it in the refresher.

Shelbi walked naked through her ship to her bedroom. The door opened. Directly in front of her was Phillip's med pod. She gazed through the clear top at his bruised and violated body and shook her head. Then she slyly smiled because they had extracted the prince and the One Mother and chaos would soon reign. No prisoner had ever been broken out of their security prison before. Two in one day was unimaginable.

"Take that, Sergoymils," she scoffed.

She walked around the end of Phillip's med pod and glanced at the One Mother's med pod. The top was glazed over for privacy and she couldn't see inside. The image of her lying on the prison bed with bruises everywhere worried Shelbi.

She shook her weary head and crawled naked in between the soft pale blue sheets on her bed. As the fog of sleep enveloped her, all she could think about was getting them home and healing them.

Shelbi was right. Chaos reigned in the dreaded prison. Electrical fires, spontaneous trash explosions, failed security cameras, and so many other things had set the prison on high alert. The master plan that Shelbi had created with the help of the Warrior Princess Elite Strategy Council had worked flawlessly thanks to many warrior princesses and princes. It would be months before the Sergoymils prison returned to near normal.

Shelbi's rescue plan started a chain of dramatic events the Sergoymils would never fully recover from. That was price they paid for messing with Shelbi MacPhadden and her elite warrior friends.

Chapter 10: The Hyperspace Journey to Safety

Lieutenant Shelbi awoke to an unfamiliar sound in her spaceship: a soft humming noise. The bed cover fell from her bare prosthetic breasts and crumpled into her naked lap, covering most of the kinky black hair sprouting between her scarred thighs.

Immediately she remembered what the hum was. At the foot of her bed was the One Mother's med pod. Beside her bed was Prince Phillip's. Both med pods admitted a low hum as they went about their job of stabilizing and repairing the two broken people they softly cradled.

She rolled out of the warm bed and looked down at the frosted lid of the One Mother's med pod shielding her from view. No one needed to see the mass of back and purple bruises inflicted by the enemy. Even her inner thighs and breasts had horrible bruises.

She padded over to look at Phillip. His med pod was clear and she could see his entire naked body. His chiselled chest rose and fell as he breathed. She gasped as she saw the number of bruises and thought what he must have gone through. Her eyes travelled down his six-pack rippling stomach. Again, more purple and black bruises, more destruction.

Her eyes continued to travel down to his limp manhood. She laughed inwardly. Finally, she had Phillip naked in her bedroom. However, looking at his bruised and torn body, all she could think about was him healing, not his alien rod rising to salute her or sliding slowly between her hot wet thighs in erotic ecstasy.

She glanced down at her own body still covered with the prosthetics. Her left breast was slightly larger than her right. Her right purple nipple was high on her breast, part of the disguise. The curly black hair between her pudgy thighs replaced her usual smooth skin. Black hair was not fun compared to her natural copper mound that usually adorn the top of the vee of her thighs. The vagina ring hanging down made her feel disgusted and angry. The enemy implanted vagina rings in the young females that worked in the prison to exploit them.

As she walked stark-naked into the bathroom, she glanced in the mirror and saw the prosthetics along her arms, making them appear more muscular and almost manlike. Her left leg was bowed and browned. She looked at the scar on the inside of her left leg where she had hidden the stem pads.

"I wonder how that red jagged scar was inflicted on the poor girl," she thought.

She had created these prosthetics to match the girl whose place she taken in prison work to rescue her Prince Phillip.

She smiled because she knew the girl and her family were safely on their way to Phillip's planet. The girl would have cosmetic surgery to align her breasts. Her nipples would be placed exactly how she wanted them. Surgery wouldn't stop the sensations; in fact, with the nerve damage repaired in her left nipple, she would have more sensation than she ever had before. Her red scar tissue would be removed and her leg straightened. Her skin would be a pale brown with a soft texture any man would love to caress. She and her family would get the royal treatment for life for service to the prince. Shelbi looked forward to meeting the girl again after she returned to the planet and the girl's surgeries were complete.

It was time to remove her own prosthetics. She walked out of the bathroom and through her bedroom into the hall. She felt the larger uneven left breast banging against her. She would be glad to return to her regular melon-sized breasts. She came to her secure room and put her palm on the pad and her eye to the telescope scanner. Her arm was pricked by a needle to take a sample of her DNA to confirm her identity. All three things were required to open this particular room on her ship. It contained highly sensitive artificial intelligence and other key items. One of those key items was the sonic wand.

When the princess elite group developed the prosthetic technology, they designed it to adhere not only to the body but actually integrate itself into several layers of the skin. It couldn't simply be ripped off. It required the sonic wand, which would disturb the molecular structure and cause it to withdraw from the skin.

The bad news was that a certain amount of heat and tingling were generated as it disengaged. Since Shelbi's extensive prosthetics covered 95% of her body, the tingling generated would be significant and definitely erotic.

She knew from her training that it would take several hours to remove the prosthetics. She took the sonic wand out of its secure place in her vault. Then, using a code only she knew, she opened the box and took it out. The technology contained within the wand would mould itself to the contours of her body, so it could cover the prosthetics regardless of what shape or size they were. It also could be attached to another surface to allow her to move her arms or reach her back without having to hold it.

Shelbi passed the wand around her left foot and moved it up the prosthetics on her left leg. By the time she'd moved up her calf to her kneecap, she was starting to sweat and pant. It felt like 1,000 tiny fingers massaging her body.

The warmth that came with it was comforting and definitely sensual.

After resting for a few minutes in the padded dark blue chair, she continued past the kneecap up to her curvy hips. The feeling the wand created on her inner thigh was sexual. In fact, Iit was designed to evoke this feeling to offset any discomfort or pain that was being caused as it retracted the prosthetic filaments from her tender skin. She began to fantasize that Phillip was caressing her leg. She imagined his soft lips travelling up her inner thighs. She thought about his caresses as they moved across her white velvet skin creating goose bumps

After finishing her left leg, she could hardly wait to start her right, but decided to do the area around her vagina and the soft mound above it.

"I really want to get rid of this brutal ring," she thought. *"It's so annoying and sensuous at the same time. If it hadn't been placed by the enemy to control the women of the planet, it would be sweet to feel it rubbing against my thighs."*

When she had inserted the ring in her prosthetic pouting vagina lips, she was initially aroused, but that quickly disappeared when she realized her prison surroundings and what the ring really represented.

As she moved the wand slowly between her thighs, she grasped the ring and pulled hard. It came away with the prosthetic pad that had been shaped around her swollen vagina lips. As she looked down at it, she exclaimed aloud, "It really is tender, like I've just gone through a round of rhythmic sex pounding. What a shame Phillip's thighs haven't created this feeling yet."

She became slightly wet and almost climaxed as she could feel the heat of the prosthetics being removed and fantasized that it was Phillip's hot wet tongue working up and down her swollen vagina lips. As the pad slid off her warm soft thighs, her copper hair reappeared. She scratched and played with it.

"Welcome back, my red furry friend!" she said aloud and laughed. "I never thought I'd be so glad to see you without a lover to take advantage of your curly redness," she said as she playfully tugged.

She paused and took an energy drink. The heat of the treatment caused a lot of sweating.

Next, she started to work on her arms beginning with her left arm.

"I'll just imagine my Phillip kissing his way up the inside of my arm as I take these prosthetics off," she thought to distract herself from the pain.

The prosthetics on the arm were actually implanted deepest to make sure they reacted exactly like her arms and would not be spotted by the enemy as the prosthetics they were.

As she worked near the top of her shoulders and under her arm, the heat in her armpit made her gasp in pain.

Just as the pain reached the worst point, it began to recede. After a short break, she started on her breasts.

"This is the part I'm really not looking forward. The warmth, especially around my nipples, is definitely going to get me close to a climax," Shelbi remarked.

Starting with the larger left prostatic breast, she held out the bosom with her left hand and used her right hand to move the wand over and around the breast tissue.

"Here it comes!" she exclaimed. "The heat on my nipple is like Phillip's hot breath. Now it feels like he's running his teeth over my nipple. The pain is just like him chewing on it. Oh my gosh, it's so wonderfully erotic."

By the time she finished with the left breast, her own beautiful ivory breast and cherry nipple were revealed. She was definitely warm and wet between her legs and it felt so good to actually relax and feel naturally sexy again. She started on her right breast, but she pulled at it too quickly and the prosthetic hadn't quite disengaged from the soft areola. It felt like her nipple was being pinched between two large fingers.

She rubbed her palm over her right nipple to ease the pain. It gave her an erotic sensation and she could feel the tension building in her body again. She couldn't stop her hands travelling down her stomach, then down the inside of her tingling thighs. She slid her hand over her hot, swollen vagina lips and felt the wonderful wetness there.

Her entire bare body had a tingling soreness to it. She couldn't stop softly rubbing back and forth on her erect clitoris to build the sensation until she could barely stand it. She then plunged her fingers deep within her vagina and stroked the red swollen lips below her copper mound.

"Phillip, yes, Phillip, yes, Phillip," she yelled.

Her entire body seized. Her legs clamped together as she buried her warm fingers into her moist vagina and felt it clutch as she climaxed over and over and over. It was a release of the sexual feeling and the pent-up energy from the battles she had been through in the past days.

Her legs trembled and shook as her climax continued for longer than usual. Finally, she lay back in the padded chair covered in sweat, her trembling thighs sticky from the sexual juices that had run down them.

Shelbi felt relaxed and happy for the first time in a long, long time. Then reality crashed her happy mood and she visualized Phillip covered in bruises and blood. She started to feel slightly guilty and then stopped.

"Wait a minute. I've earned that climax. I deserve that climax. And later on, I'm going to do it again!" Shelbi said smiling.

She needed a shower to wash the final residue of the prosthetics off and clean herself.

"Someday, my prince will come! Yes, and it will be inside my wonderful pulsating vagina."

Chapter 11: The Homestead Rewards

The Estrada personal environmental car was in full alarm mode as it travelled down the country road. Shelbi relaxed in the driver's seat with the firm belief that the Sergoymils would not try anything so soon after her momentous victory rescuing the One Mother and Prince Phillip.

She marvelled as she looked out the windows at the amazing trees and the rolling countryside. Just like back on Earth, some trees were leafy green, some dark green pine-like, and others had yellow and orange leaves on their branches.

She reviewed in her mind exactly what today was about. She had let Ben and Beth Saunders know that she was coming to the homestead to greet them. She also told them she didn't want this to be a formal affair, that she just wanted to meet them and have a short tour of her new homestead.

When the One Mother deeded her the homestead plus the additional land, she had been taken aback, but the One Mother was adamant. Shelbi had saved her life and the life of the Prince Phillip, her godson. It was the least she could do, she said. This made Shelbi the first off-world person to be included in the planet's homestead generation.

She thought about the fact that Phillip was going to come to the homestead today as a friend, not on an official visit. He was going to help her as she walked around the homestead look for areas that could be improved in the design. He also agreed to go for a horse ride in the afternoon out on the homestead's land.

Shelbi's mind went back many months before. She remembered his shirtless chest. Her nipples hardened as she remembered her breasts rubbing against the hair on his chest, his muscular arms holding her. She remembered the smell of his manly body and the softness of his warm lips as he kissed her neck. She could almost remember the hardness of his manhood pressed against her bare belly. The sound of an alarm brought her back to reality.

As the car neared the entrance to her new homestead, she noted that the people in the fields seemed friendly and waved at her. She had specifically told Ben she didn't want a big welcoming ceremony. They could have a more formal one after she had met Ben and they decided on a date together. She was here to meet them and have an informal luncheon with them.

As she rolled up to the front of the homestead mansion, she noticed two people standing in full uniform on the steps. She knew from the photographs that this was Ben and Beth Saunders who had been running the homestead for a number of years.

As she stopped, a tall homesteader ran up to open the door for her. Emerging, she said, "Thank you."

"My honour, Homesteader MacPhadden," said the black-haired young man.

Shelbi walked over to Ben and extended her hand. "Fore Person Ben Saunders, it is a pleasure to meet you."

"Thank you, Homesteader MacPhadden. It's indeed a pleasure to meet you."

Beth and Shelbi exchanged greetings, though Beth appeared tense, smiled slightly, and said, "Homesteader MacPhadden, it is a pleasure to meet you."

Shelbi understood. They had lived on the homestead for many years and now they had a new unknown, untried, and alien homesteader. This would make any sane person nervous.

Beth turned slightly and said to Shelbi, "I'd like to show you your new home now."

There was a slight tremble in her voice and Shelbi began to understand just how nervous Beth really was.

As they got to the top of the stairs, Shelbi spoke up. "Beth, I'd really like to have a cup of tea before going on a tour. Perhaps we could go into the kitchen and talk while you're making it. Ben, it would be great if you could join us."

Ben seemed to hesitate but being a true professional, he turned immediately and said, "Yes, of course, Homesteader Shelbi MacPhadden."

They arrived in the kitchen and Beth turned to Shelbi nervously. "I'm sorry, this is the One Mother's logo on the teapot. We haven't had a chance to talk to you about your logo or new design."

Shelbi smiled and said, "Not to worry, Beth. These are all things we can work out together."

Beth seemed to hesitate as she realized Shelbi had just said they would be working together. *"Perhaps the future is not so bleak,"* she thought with a little hope for the first time since they had learned of their new homesteader.

While Beth made the tea, Shelbi quietly asked some questions. She learned that Ben Saunders had come to the homestead with his parents and two brothers when he was three years old. As he grew, he learned about the various jobs on the farm and had done them all. He then went to the University of Tauro with a scholarship from the One Mother where he had learned about homesteader management, financing, and other ways to run and improve the homestead.

She also learned how he had met his wife, Beth. He had been part of the marching band and Beth had been the head of the colour guard. They had become fast friends. Soon, Ben had fallen in love with Beth's brown hair and freckles. She had fallen for his chiselled jaw, manly shoulders, strong arms, and blue eyes. They'd come to the homestead and moved into this house when Ben was promoted to fore person.

The house had five bedrooms. The master bedroom for Ben and Beth, three bedrooms for their three children – two boys and a girl – and a fifth bedroom that was used as an office. Shelbi also learned that Beth was the accountant and purchasing manager. She took care of all the books and made sure that they balanced at the end of each fiscal year, ensured supplies were in stock, seed was purchased, and there was enough food for the galley where many of the farm hands had lunch.

When the tea was ready, Shelbi suggested they move into the living room. She sat down in one of the two chairs facing the couch. Ben and Beth still appeared a little nervous as they sat down facing Shelbi. Beth continued to refer to the homestead as Shelbi's house. Shelbi decided to address this emotional item first.

"Ben and Beth, I've had some time to think about the homestead and my responsibilities. I've also spent some time talking and thinking about your responsibilities. As you know, Prince Phillip is a friend of mine."

At the mention of his name, Ben and Beth quickly looked at each other and the tension rose noticeably in the room.

"What we are about to discuss is something I've talked about with Prince Phillip and the One Mother. They've agreed with my approach pending discussions with you. I would like to talk to you about the house that you've occupied for 21 years first."

Beth looked at Shelbi with tears starting to form in her eyes. "We understand, Homesteader MacPhadden. It's your home and we will be moving out. We understand that's how it is and we're fine with that."

She stopped talking and gulped a couple of times. Ben reached out his left hand and took Beth's right hand in his, sadly realizing tradition dictated that the homesteader owned the house and the fore person did not. Shelbi looked at them and started to speak quickly.

"Ben and Beth, I'm going to give you this home."

Ben and Beth each blurted out, "But how can we afford it? It has a huge mortgage. How will we pay for it? Where will you live?"

Shelbi remained calm. "Ben and Beth, I need you to help me so my first gift to you is this home. It's been your family home for many years and I want you to keep it. Part of my gift is to pay off the mortgage, so you don't have to worry about that. And yes, Beth, as the accountant here, that may not seem like a good idea, but that's the way we do things for people we trust in my world."

A tear rolled down Beth's cheek as she looked at Ben and clutched his hand tightly. Ben looked between Beth and Shelbi and clearly wasn't sure what to say.

"I'm giving you this house as a gift. I believe you've earned it with your service to the One Mother. I believe you will be a great help to me in the future," Shelbi assured them.

Ben seemed to find his voice. "I'm astonished and very pleased. Thank you, Homesteader MacPhadden," and he bowed slightly to her.

"As to where I will live, I would like to build a new home on the homestead that fits my needs. I don't need five bedrooms but I do need a large conference room that we can use for our meetings. We'll talk about the details later. It's one of the many new projects I want you to take on."

Shelbi reached down and picked up her teacup. She let the silence unfold as the two of them had taken in a tremendous amount of information. They had assumed they would have to leave the house. They had assumed their children would be uprooted. Now one of their biggest dreams had come true. Not only did they not have to leave the house, their children could stay and they wouldn't have the crippling debt of trying to do it alone.

Shelbi then continued, "I want to talk about my ideas for my homestead. I started some things in motion and, pending final discussions with you, we can complete them.

The first one is Grand Master Machinery Incorporated. I have a tentative agreement with them to supply us with their latest technology for a fee of 100,000 drones a year."

Beth looked startled, "That's a very big fee to pay!"

Shelbi smiled. "Beth, that's not a fee we have to pay. That's the fee they will pay us."

Beth frowned, afraid she had offended the new homesteader, then she quickly said, "I'm sorry I misunderstood, Homesteader MacPhadden."

Shelbi continued to smile and said, "I understand. Additionally, I've talked to Techno Aggro Inc. They also will be paying us 100,000 drones each year to have their technology on the homestead. In return, we will provide them with feedback on how it works, doesn't work, or could be improved. Also, once a quarter, they're allowed to bring people here for a tour. They can see how the equipment is used on a real homestead and talk to the operators. We will work out the details later, if this sounds agreeable to you."

Ben spoke up. "Let me see if I understand this. We get new technology, they pay us 200,000 drones per year, and we have to accommodate a tour once a quarter."

Shelbi said, "Yes, that is exactly right, if it makes sense to you, Ben."

Again, Ben and Beth were startled but managed to control their emotions. Ben smiled and said, "This is another dream come true. Having the latest technology from the two most advanced companies on the planet, well, we just can't thank you enough."

Shelbi picked up her cup and took another sip of hot black tea. Shelbi spoke softly but with some force.

"Ben, the One Mother has given us an additional 150 quatrains."

In her mind, Shelbi was converting one quatrain to 1.55 acres. This made the homestead fairly large, not the largest on the planet, but definitely a good size.

"The additional area is beside the existing homestead and is just raw land at the moment," Shelbi said. "I've had discussions and made arrangements with the University of Tauro and they will be building a model farm on the property at their expense. Each semester, they will send students to work the farm, learn, and gain co-op time. They will pay a fee for the use of the property."

Shelbi stopped talking for a moment and could see Ben processing the information. "I've also talked to Toronto University and they also wish to build a farm on part of the property and arrange for their students to work here each semester as part of their co-op program. They will also pay a fee to use the property." Shelbi stopped talking again to check their reaction. It appeared positive but she wanted to ask the question. "Ben, does this make sense to you?"

"Yes, this sounds amazing! How much land do you think they will be taking over?" The nervousness seemed to have left his voice and he was more in thinking leadership mode.

"To start with, I said they could each have 5 to 7 quatrains. However, I said the final negotiation on size would be with you. After all, you're going to be managing this."

Shelbi could see them thinking about the responsibility and workload that was coming. They were now going to take on two mega corporations and their technology, two new farms, additional co-op students, additional permanent staff, plus new homes. This was going to be a tremendous amount of extra effort.

"This means a tremendous amount of new responsibility. Do you have any concerns?" Shelbi asked.

Ben appeared thoughtful and unsure what to say. He finally looked at Shelbi and said, "Speaking for Beth and myself, if that's what you need, Homesteader, we will make it happen."

Shelbi could see the tension in both of them. They were concerned and worried about fulfilling her wishes.

Shelbi calmly unfolded her legs, and put her hands in her lap, and said, "I have more news that I believe is positive." Shelbi stood up and said, "Ben, stand please." Looking at Beth, she said, "Beth, would you stand too, please?"

She then walked around the wooden coffee table to stand in front of Ben. Tension filled the air. Ben was clearly concerned. Beth was emotionally charged. What was their homesteader thinking? What was this all about!

Shelbi reached out her right hand, put it on Ben's right shoulder, and said, "Fore Person Ben, from this moment on, you will be known as Lord Person Ben Theodore Saunders."

Beth collapsed on the couch with her hand against her mouth and a tear running down her cheek. She was thinking, *"This is more than I could ever have hoped for my wonderful Ben."*

Ben appeared stunned. Quickly, he responded, "Homesteader MacPhadden, I'm pleased to be your Lord Person." He then turned quickly and Beth leapt off the couch and into his muscular arms. She was softly crying salty tears of joy against his cheek.

Beth turned around and bowed to Homesteader Shelbi. "Homesteader MacPhadden, you've made me one of the happiest women on the planet today. My Ben deserves it and I'm so pleased that he has been given this honour," Beth gushed.

Then, to the astonishment of Ben and Beth, Shelbi reached out her right hand and put it on Beth's right shoulder. "Beth Saunders, from this moment forward, you will be known as the Lady Person Anne Elizabeth Saunders."

Ben grabbed Beth from behind and held her up. She was stunned.

"Is this for real?" Beth finally said.

Shelbi looked at Beth with a smile and said, "Yes, Beth. You are now a Lady Person."

"Homesteader MacPhadden, I'm pleased to be your Lady Person," Beth said, quickly remembering the formal thank you required to complete the first round of the oaths.

Beth spun around and grabbed Ben. They were both crying and hugging each other. Shelbi quietly backed off and walked to the front door to leave them to celebrate in the intimate way only a loving husband and wife can.

Suddenly they recovered and realized what had just happened. Ben raced to the front door and stammered, "I – I- I apologize. I'm sorry, we were just so taken aback. I'm so sorry!"

Shelbi put her hand softly on his left arm and said, "I knew this was going to be a lot for you to take in. The emotion you've both shown is exactly why I want you to be part of my homestead, Lord Saunders."

Shelbi returned to her chair and sat down. "I now need you to listen to this next part. It's equally important to some of what is going on today. Are you ready for more good news?"

Ben looked at Beth and they said in unison, "Yes!"

Shelbi continued, "This is going to be a lot of work for one lord person. Ben, I'm giving you the authority to hire three fore persons who will report to you. Beth, as Lady Person, I'm giving you the authority to hire two fore persons who will report directly to you. I've given you a tremendous amount of new responsibility and you're going to need help. After you've had a chance to think about it and plan, if you actually need more people, we can talk about that. There are still a lot of details to work on, but don't worry about funding, as I said."

Shelbi appeared lost in thought for a moment then said, "Prince Phillip Yerffej is nearly here. He's coming for lunch and to be part of the ceremony when I place the Lord Person bars on both of you. He's not coming officially as the prince. He's coming as my friend to help me understand how things are done on this world."

Ben and Beth shot up. Shelbi laughed. "Now, now, you two have a lot to talk about. Just relax. I'm going to go sit on the porch until Phillip arrives. And, please remember this is not an official visit."

Shelbi walked away to leave them to talk. Having covered many of her official duties and set many things in motion, the tension ebbed from her body. She was looking forward to a horse ride out to the waterfall after lunch with Phillip.

Maybe, just maybe, they would explore more virgin territory. Shelbi sat alone on the porch and thought about Phillip's powerful erect manhood pressing hard against her soft belly and how much she wanted it between her moist thighs.

Chapter 12: Waterfall Hot Caresses

Phillip's chiselled face felt warm. The sun was beating down on his body and the beautiful chestnut horse he sat on with the heat of the early afternoon.

A river ran through much of the northeast part of the homestead and Shelbi had spotted the waterfall while riding around the property. She had been eager to take Phillip there ever since.

A smile turned his full, manly lips up as he watched the wooden front door open and Shelbi stride out in her brown riding boots, tight black riding pants, and shimmering pale blue blouse.

"What amazing, sensuous legs she has," the prince thought as he watched her walk straight to her horse being held by a groomsman. *"I can't wait to run my fingers over her bare flesh..."*

"My prince, I can hear you!" Shelbi interrupted as she smiled and looked at him.

He laughed, realizing he had not blocked the mind link.

"You're about to get a lesson in what a warrior princess elite can do when caressing a big alien like yourself!" Shelbi thought.

The groomsman helped her straddle the pale yellow palomino horse that Phillip had picked out for her. She felt the stretch in her inner thighs as she spread her long legs in the saddle. The horse was bigger than those on her home planet and really stretched her legs wide. She was glad she had done some warm-up exercises.

As the horses walked on, Shelbi and Phillip left the established homestead and moved out into the raw land the One Mother had provided. The rolling uncapped hills were lush with green vegetation and the occasional groups of red and yellow wildflowers. Although the tension was high between them, they idly chattered about the landscape, wildflowers, and anything to keep their minds off the lust that was making both their bodies quiver.

When they arrived at the waterfall, Shelbi got off the horse and gazed longingly at the crystal clear water flowing over the beautiful red granite cliff into a pool below.

"While you're surveying the beautiful landscape, I will set the horses up so they can roam and feed. I also have the super blanket part of your new technology gift."

Shelbi laughed. "I didn't think about bringing a blanket. I'm glad one of us is thinking how to avoid a grass rash on my skin."

Phillip stuck a corral spike in the ground and the horses ambled off. He took the tiny super blanket out of its container, pushed the blue tab, and marvelled as it expanded into a 10-foot by 10-foot soft brown blanket he could lay on the ground.

Shelbi sat down quickly on the blanket, pulling her riding boots off. Next, she stripped off her socks and rolled up the legs of her riding pants. She then strode down and walked into the water. Phillip stood and just admired her womanly form as her broad hips swayed when she walked down the slight hill and into the warm water.

As she stood feeling the warm water run against the bare skin of her legs, she reached into her side pocket and pulled out the brown lens case. She popped the golden lenses in. She had been wearing the golden lenses now for several months and she was able to use them for hours at a time.

She saw the amazing colours swirling around the water and then she turned to take in Phillip's full colour for the first time. The electric reds, oranges, and yellows swirling around him were even more vibrant where his ridged rod strained the front of his form-fitting black riding pants. She could only imagine what it would look like when he was naked.

Shelbi turned and started to walk back to the blanket as Phillip began removing his shirt. Shelbi looked at his magnificent broad shoulders tapering down to his narrow hips. His dark auburn brown muscled skin rippled with each movement, causing his red and yellow colours to swirl from his manly nipples. Her mind drifted back to the last time she'd seen his naked chest at her home with her bare breasts crushed against his powerful abs.

Phillip blocked his mind so Shelbi couldn't hear his thoughts. He had watched her walk up and had seen the change in the colours as the electric reds and oranges had swirled around her body when her eyes devoured his figure. His keen eyes noted her nipples. He saw how stiff they were beneath the fabric of her pale blue blouse.

When her blouse fell to the ground showing her creamy skin underneath and the most amazingly erotic lacy pale blue bra, his mind control slipped. *"My God, I can't wait to rain hot kisses over those amazing breasts. I will pluck your nipples with my warm tongue and sharp white teeth till she begs me to stop."*

Shelbi smiled and thought back, *"I heard that. I want to pay the same attention to your manly parts, not just your nipples but that area that's happy to see me."*

She reached behind her and undid the clasp of her blue frilly bra. She held it in place with her right hand and used her left hand to move the satin blue straps off each bare shoulder. Then with a wicked smile, she removed both cups from her breasts. Her rosy nipples were fully alert. The electric reds burst out from each erection.

Phillip was now clearly in discomfort as his manhood forced its way up the front of his riding pants. He slipped his hand inside and undid the zipper. Shelbi realized that he had gone commando and didn't want to catch himself on his zipper.

"Good job. We don't want to damage it before I stroke it with my tongue," she thought.

He pulled his pants off, so did Shelbi. Standing half naked in her blue bikini underwear, her breath quickened as she stared at her magnificent naked prince.

They walked quickly toward each other. Then he was crushing her soft full breasts against his hard chest. He could feel his hardness pressing like a stiff rod against her white belly. Her copper mound prickled the bottom of it and set another wave of excitement through his thighs.

Shelbi's hands moved towards her bikini briefs to take them off, but Phillip quickly stopped her.

"The pleasure is all mine," he said.

She could feel the heat of his palms against her hips. She pushed her hips out slightly from his naked body, but kept her warm breasts crushed against his chest. He slowly slipped the panties down her silky bare legs, running his thumbs over her broad thighs and down the outside of her long slim legs, taking her panties with them. When he got them down to Shelbi's heels, his hand grabbed the back of one calf and held it up. Shelbi looked and saw the electrical red and yellow colours swirling around her leg mix with his hand and felt the warmth as he touched her calf. Then he lifted her other bare leg and slid the panties off. The amazing red, yellow, and orange colours swirling around increased the sexual feeling that was already vibrating her body.

Phillip swept her off her feet and held her in his arms. First, his tongue caressed the edges of her lips. She parted her lips and his tongue flashed in to caress her warm tongue. He started raining kisses on the soft skin of her throat and across her ample right breast. His lips met her peaking red nipple and she could feel his naked ridged manhood pressing against her as she lay across his arms.

He continued to kiss her velvet belly and when he reached her copper mound, the electric red and orange colours exploded. Then that magnificent thing happened when Shelbi was pleasuring herself: a purple colour started to roll around her copper mound over his hips. Phillip jerked his head up, staring at the purple lines of electricity smouldering across her copper mound.

"Oh my God!" he gasped. "This is amazing. Only the people related to the legendary Warrior Princess Shanii can create purple electricity. You really are the warrior princess!" he said as he dragged his tongue across her copper mound and between her sensuous legs.

Phillip's legs started to tremble with the passion he was feeling for Shelbi's bare body. His manhood was as large as it had ever been and he began to wonder if Shelbi could really take it all in her small, wet human vagina. He set Shelbi down on the blanket and stared at her for a moment.

Shelbi quickly released her right leg and rolled him on to the ground. She rolled under and over him, rubbing her breasts against his skin while her soft hands explored the insides of his thighs. Phillip almost exploded. Never had he felt the passion and erotic excitement of any woman before like he did with Shelbi.

Her lips travelled across his chest and she began nipping his left nipple with her front teeth. The prince's hand roamed down her back and across her backside. Her vagina lips were now soaking wet and pouting with passion.

Phillip's manhood shot upwards as he rolled on his side. He reached into the back pocket of his black pants and pulled out a small piece of round clear film. He laid it on the head of his enormous erection. The clear film expanded and flowed down the pulsating shaft, covering the red veins and the top of his balls. In her mind, Shelbi heard the prince's words, *"As protector of women, I always wear a sheath for protection."*

Shelbi answered, *"I have my own vagina coated protection."*

"I know, but I'm trying to help all men on the planet understand how important protected sex is and the One Mother knows I want to have sex with you!" he said as he rolled quickly across the space between their naked bodies.

Shelbi ran her fingers over his stomach and up to his moist abs then began to palm his erect nipples. He mirrored her, running his fingers across the velvet skin of her belly after tugging at her copper mound. He too began to palm her hard nipples, shooting red orange and yellow lines of electricity between them.

"Now I'm going to taste that honey nectar between your magnificent thighs," he said, marvelling at the swirling electrical colours.

Shelbi spread her legs as wide as they had been when she rode the horse. The warmth of the sun on her skin and the slight prickle of stubble on the prince's chin on her inner sensitive thighs almost made her climax.

"If you go much slower, I'm going to orgasm by myself," she panted.

"I want to make you cum more times this afternoon than you ever have before," he said, sending shots of purple and yellow rolling up from between her thighs, across her flat trembling stomach, and over her full breasts.

His tongue reached her swollen vagina lips and lightly caressed them as the tension mounted in her body, waiting for him to plunge inside.

"I'm going to just keep playing with your lips until you've climaxed at least twice," he said.

The tension pushed Shelbi over the edge. She clutched her trembling legs around his head and came with a mighty roar, shaking her body, and making her breasts dance as the electric reds and purple swirled around them.

He released his head from her clutched, shaking thighs and continued sucking her pouting vagina lips.

"Your nectar is so delicious!"

His hand reached under her backside and raised her off the blanket as his tongue continued to dart up and down her quivering wet vagina lips.

The electrical reds and yellows rolling around her thighs and the occasional purple shooting up her stomach were so erotic that she could feel the tension mounting again. Before she could stop herself, she grabbed her hands and plunged them into his hair, trying to force his tongue inside her eager wet channel. He pushed his head back and kept his tongue working on her lips until the tension was too much once again and her legs began to quiver as she climaxed.

In one of those elite moves Phillip hadn't quite got used to, she pushed at his shoulder, flipped him on his back, and began kissing his neck as her pouting hot vagina lips rode up and down on his erect pulsating manhood. His hands roamed over her back and outside her thighs in eager anticipation and excitement.

She planted her bare feet beside his firm muscular thighs and raised herself above his naked body. Reaching her hand down, she began to stroke his hard manhood. She realized how thick and hard it was and wondered if she really could stretch to take it inside her.

Smiling with lust at him, she thought, *"Let's just try it!"*

Rubbing the large purple head back and forth on her puffy wet vagina lips once again, the erotic emotions overtook her as she collapsed on his chest. Another climax trembled through her body. Then she slowly began to straddle him.

"Oh my God," she thought. *"It is so enormous, it is stretching me to my limit. He feels so good filling me up."*

"Shelbi, you feel so magnificent clamping around me," he thought.

His next thought was to himself, blocked from Shelbi, *"I hope I'm not hurting her!"*

As if in answer to his thoughts Shelbi said, "Your manhood is so huge, you're straining my inner channel, but the pleasure is much greater than the pain."

Finally, Shelbi had taken his erect manhood fully inside her smouldering vagina. Her love juices continued to roll down her canal and out over his body, making his thighs as sticky as hers.

As she lay down on his chest, crushing her nipples and breasts into the warmth of his chest and his hard abs, he slipped his hand behind her head and her bottom. She tensed, knowing what was coming.

In his own elite move, he quickly turned her over, protecting her head, and crushed her body against him. Then moving her legs outside his thighs, he began to slowly move in and out of her wonderful warm womanhood. Her slipperiness made it easy, although she still felt his enormous girth rubbing and stretching the sides of her hot channel.

She pulled her legs up so the heels of her feet were clamping his amazingly firm buttocks. She watched as the colours rolled around on the electric reds, electric yellow, and then the amazing electrical purple that was now engulfing her belly, her breasts, his chest, and his ridged manhood as it moved in and out of the space between her soaking wet thighs.

Her breasts moved up and down, rubbing her hot erect nipples against his chest to create even more stimulation as his rhythm continued. Then she plucked at his ridged nipples. A moan escaped from his mouth. The sun added to their heat and both of them were now covered in rivulets of sweat.

"You're amazing. You're so wet. You're so hot," he thought.

Then his rhythm increased and Shelbi wrapped her arms around his body, pining herself tight to his naked skin. They came at the same time. Shelbi screamed in ancient animal lust. Her body was shaking and she could feel Phillip exploding deep inside her. Amazingly, his condom still managed to give her the feeling of the heat of his hot alien cum.

As he started to slide out of her, she dug her heels into his backside, forcing him to slow down.

"Not yet, my prince, not yet," Shelbi moaned. "I don't want to let go of this feeling. Besides, I'm still trembling from our climax."

Finally, Shelbi cuddled into his sweat-covered arms as he removed his manhood from her hot sore channel. She loved a man who cuddled and clearly Phillip loved to feel her warm body against his. Her hands roamed over his chest, sliding in slick sweat, which felt so deliciously erotic.

Phillip's left hand ran up and down her back covered in perspiration. They lay naked in the hot afternoon sun on the soft blanket with their fingers exploring each other's body.

He began to kiss her shoulders and his lips roamed down the mounds of her breasts. Her hands were busy roaming down to his rippled stomach, searching out his manhood, which was becoming hard again.

They spent much of the afternoon naked on the blanket, exploring different ways to make love to one another, and learning how to satisfy one another.

Finally, they realized the time had come to return to their professional duties and private challenges. They walked hand in hand naked down to the water. As they stood facing each other, Phillip scooped up water and washed Shelbi's body. He ran his hands over her pale thighs, her warm hips, across her breasts, washing the sweat off with the cool water. As his hands began to wash her thighs inside, Shelbi shuddered and grabbed his hands as his fingers caressed her southern lips. The electrical purple colour swirled around her nakedness.

Using his thumb softy on her swollen sore nub, he managed to bring her to another strong body-shaking climax. As she trembled in the throes of ecstasy, Shelbi almost fell to her knees. Phillip's strong arms held her up, pressing her cool bare breasts against his body. She finally regained control of her limbs and started to wash his chest.

"My prince, you appear to be saluting me again!"

"Yes, my princess. I will always salute you this way!" he said looking down at the yellows and reds swirling around his manhood.

She began to caress the hard rod, feeling the pounding veins reacting to her fingers. Then she moved her mouth down to the purple head and ran her tongue around and around as if she was licking an ice cream cone. As her fingers continued to caress it, she locked her lips on the shaft and began to slide up and down, sucking and licking. Moans began to escape his lips, as he knew how this pleasure would end. He could feel the tension rising in his legs. At the last moment, he screamed out in ecstasy.

Shelbi took her warm red lips off his purple tip and continued to stroke him. She watched as his princely essence shot out into the clear water of the brook. The seed flow slowed down and she quickly clamped her lips over his manhood to drink in his essence one last time.

He stepped away shakily. "If you keep this up, you'll have to throw me over the horse," Phillip said with a mix of amusement and weariness.

Their colours seemed to be fading. Shelbi realized her lenses were starting to dissolve, but that didn't change the heat of the moment any less for her weary, sore body. Phillip sat down in the water and Shelbi washed his back and shoulders. He stopped her when she started to work on his thighs.

"I really have found my match. I've never stopped a woman before, but I think I might just die if you do that again!" he said with a smile and a weariness that met Shelbi's thoughts.

They walked back across the grass and lay down on the blanket, letting the sun dry them off before getting dressed. As they rode back, Phillip said, "I don't think I've had saddle soreness like this ever before."

Shelbi thought, *"This ache might stop me from walking naturally. Hopefully I'll be better by the time we get back to the homestead."*

The prince laughed and thought, *"I can hear you, my sexy princess."*

Shelbi hoped there would be more days like this. He was such a wonderful man to make love to. Little did she know just how soon that would happen.

Chapter 13: University Ceremonial Day

Shelbi glanced at the knife-edge crease on her right-hand pant leg. She smiled at how regimental and professional she looked.

She slipped on the short green jacket and buttoned it, noticing how it accented her narrow waist. It was designed specifically for functionality but took on a sensuality on her body. The homesteader ceremonial white bone knife that the One Mother had given her previously was tucked into her black leather belt.

Shelbi saw the major bars on the military uniform hanging in her closet. It reminded her of the ceremony several days before when she had been promoted from lieutenant to major thanks to her service to the One Mother and the prince by helping them escape from the Sergoymils prison.

This was an important day for her and the people of her homestead. The One Mother was officially turning over the homestead to Major Shelbi MacPhadden. The well-scripted historical ceremony would last for several hours. Shelbi would be front and centre for most of it.

Prince Phillip would be there as part of the ceremony since he represented the king and queen. Additionally, he was the head of the military force that defended all the homesteaders.

As she looked in the full-length mirror, she thought back to how she had started her day. Knowing the prince was there for the next three days, she had decided to work on arousing him. She knew they would go back to their waterfall. She wanted him primed for the few hours they had making passionate love together.

As she stepped out of the hot shower, she had stood in front of the full-length mirror in her bathroom suite. Her slender fingers had intertwined the red hair of her mound above the vee of her white thighs. She could feel the electricity and warmth roaming down her bare legs. She had then slowly drawn the soft tips of her fingers across the white skin of her stomach. As she caressed her own skin, she felt the tingle swirl and rise up and flutter across her jutting breasts. Aware now of her body colours, she saw the electric oranges and reds start to swirl.

She cupped her breasts and squeezed. The electric orange and red colours were swirling and she brought her left palm up to rotate around her pink erect nipple. She felt the warmth spread even more and the tension started to build in her trembling legs as her climax was imminent. She watched the sliver of electric purple colour roll up from between her hot thighs, across her tingling stomach, and around her breasts to explode off her tingling perky nipples.

She had expected to stop there, but she imagined Phillip's naked body lying stretched out beside her. Shelbi could sense his strong caresses running up the side of her bare thigh. Her own fingers began to explore the wetness between her eager thighs. Her clitoris was throbbing.

Using the tips of her fingers on her rigid, tender clitoris, she began to imagine Phillip's tongue teasing at her bud. Two fingers of her right hand caressed her swollen vaginal lips and continued to build the tension. She leaned against the countertop as she rode the wave of pleasure that exploded as her fingers worked between her moist thighs. She smiled again. She wanted to share this happiness with Phillip.

She shook her head and came back to the moment as she looked at the uniform's reflection in the mirror in her bedroom. The green uniform with the yellow stripes and black piping was perfect. The One Mother's uniforms for the homestead had been a light grey jacket over dark grey pants. Shelbi had embraced the greenness of the earth around and added the yellow stripes to signify excitement and the power of the sun. The black piping set it off as a unique uniform for this homestead. She strode outside and waited for the One Mother's group to arrive.

Shelbi had carefully studied the handover ceremony to understand exactly what was to happen today. She knew the various speeches she would have to deliver. She had also worked with her lord persons, since they would also be a significant part of the ceremony. The One Mother's lord person, whom all her homestead lord persons reported to, was going to be part of the ceremony and would present the Earth rod from the One Mother to Shelbi's lord person.

The Earth rod was carved from a tree that had been on the property for over 200 years. The tree had fallen down due to age and weather, and lay fallow for many years. When the One Mother set up the homestead originally, she had a strong branch from it carved as her homestead rod. It would appear at many ceremonies representing Shelbi's homesteaders and their unique connection to the land and the forest.

The next three days at the homestead were filled with proud old traditions and important cultural ceremonies. It started with the handover ceremony. On the second day, the University of Toronto would formally announce their launch of a campus on the homestead. The ceremony would involve a number of speeches in the morning. An elaborate lunch had been planned by the university in a marquee. The centrepiece would be a model of the campus they were going to build. There was a horse show in the afternoon. One of the things that the university focused on and studied was Arbel show horses, a breed that they had helped develop and train.

The third day would be for the University of Tauro. They would also host an elaborate ceremony with speeches. A luncheon would showcase a scale model of the new their campus. The afternoon included their award-winning school band, Hilltoppers Drum Corps, doing a marching and manoeuvring show. With over 150 students participating, Shelbi was eagerly anticipating the colourful and elaborate show, as they had won many local and national awards. They were including an original piece that they had specifically for this campus. It had both original music and drill manoeuvres. It would become the university's theme for all sporting and major events.

The last part of the third day made Shelbi smile late at night when she thought about it. Phillip was staying over for all three days and said he wanted to go back to the waterfall with her. They both knew they would be able to take advantage of their burning passion. Those moments were rare for them.

The One Mother's handover ceremony went well with everybody delivering speeches without a hitch. Many people from Shelbi's homestead had showed up initially in the One Mother's grey uniforms to honour their past. After Shelbi's lord persons had received the homestead rod, those who wanted to could change into the new green and yellow uniforms.

Shelbi noticed some of the people had remained in their double grey uniform. She made a note to check if they were happy staying in the new homestead or if they would rather be transferred to one of the others the One Mother still owned.

After lunch, there was a lull in the conversation for both her and the prince. They had touched briefly in their mind link and discussed several things. Now it was Shelbi's turn to remember her time after her shower this morning and share that with the prince.

She touched his mind and said, *"I have a little treat for you."*

"Should I be nervous?" he asked.

"Absolutely," Shelbi teased.

She pulled the vision of her standing naked in front of the mirror with the water dripping slowly off her breasts and thighs. She remembered running her soft fingers through her copper mound, tugging at it slightly, and feeling the arousal of the moment.

"I hope this is not going to go much further," he thought.

"Actually, it's going all the way," she thought.

She continued to remember running her fingers up her flat stomach and feeling the tips of her fingers sending sensations throughout her body. Shelbi could see the electric purple colour swirling around her wet naked body and exploding off her pert pink nipples.

"I'm beginning to sweat, among other things," he thought as his pants stretched around his erection.

"The best is yet to come," Shelbi thought.

She continued to remember cupping her left breast, working on her pink nipple, and then the magic electric purple colour running up from between her burning thighs to jump off both her erect nipples.

"Shelbi, I will pay you back!"

"I'm expecting more than just payback, my prince."

The image of her fingers plunging between her thighs was interrupted by someone asking her a question and it broke the link to the prince. She could see him physically reacting. Little did she know how he would get her back.

Later that night, Phillip headed to the shower after a full day of being out in the sun. As he grabbed the soap and began to run it over his abs, he began to think of the image Shelbi had shared of her naked body and what she had done with her fingers. He soaped up his muscular thighs and caressed his manhood until it was rock hard, thinking about her body and what he wanted to do it over and over again. As he lathered up his manhood and ran his hands up and down, he thought more and more of what she had shown him in their mind connection.

When he began to see the purple rising between her naked thighs, his pace became faster and faster. His left hand pinched his nipples as his right hand continued its rhythm up and down his stiff rod. Finally, he pressed his left hand against the wall as his right hand reached maximum rhythm. As he climaxed and released his seed into the shower, he marvelled at how the simple thought of Shelbi's naked body could make him orgasm so hard. His legs were shaking slightly as he continued to milk his pulsating rod that contained more semen than he expected.

He smiled. He knew exactly how he would start his payback for the sexy Shelbi. He had two full days to share his body and slippery rod gymnastics with her!

Chapter 14: Princess University Celebration

As Phillip buttoned up his black formal shirt, he noticed his six-pack abs had finally returned after weeks of training and working out. His stomach and chest muscles were severely damaged when he was in prison. With some reconstructive surgery and encouragement from Shelbi, he had continued training to return to his previous toned form.

He thought about how Shelbi's kindness had also provided some nanotechnology that helped increase a woman's breast size. Shelbi had realized after working with some of the warriors in his elite team that women suffer the same damage as men in the chest area. She had taken some technology she had learned and helped develop it so women could have their breasts reconstructed, not with dramatic painful surgery but with nanotechnology that was much easier for them to take.

While originally set up for female warriors, it had quickly drawn attention from other women outside the military. Phillip and Shelbi had set up clinics through a business the prince had established for medical procedures, and agreed that 20% of the profits would go to Shelbi. She reinvested it back into her homestead as another source of income. Her lord persons had been pleased to see another source of income, but very surprised when they realized the amount after the first three months.

"Focus on today," Phillip said. "I have to deliver an acceptance speech to set this university project in place."

His thoughts drifted to Shelbi again and how he was going to get back at her for taunting him with images of her fiery mound, plus the swirling electric purple colour exploding off her stiff cherry nipples. He closed his dark brown eyes for a minute to remember the wonderful sexy images. How delightful and erotic they were.

Shelbi was also putting on her formal green shirt. Before she buttoned it, she looked at her lacy bra. She remembered bending over to lower her breast into the lacy green bra cups and thinking about Phillip's soft hands. "I wish you were caressing them now, my love," she murmured.

After slipping on the matching lacy green underwear, she glanced in the full-length mirror and thought, "*Nice figure. I need to see my electric colours.*"

She moved to the box that held sets of her golden lenses. By now she could wear them all day and not be overwhelmed by the constant assault of rainbow colours all around her.

Shelbi continued to get dressed in her homesteader green outfit. She thought about her acceptance speech as part of the ceremony the University of Toronto was providing today. She also decided spontaneously that after lunch, she would go down to the temporary corral area and just look at the magnificent brown, black, and white Arbel horses the university had brought. She knew the afternoon horse performance would be exciting and interesting. Caressing their soft warm hides and smelling their rich leathery fragrance would add to the enjoyment of the ceremony.

The morning went by without a hitch. This was the largest project this university had done in the past 10 years. They were extremely thankful that Shelbi had selected their project for her homestead.

After lunch, Shelbi went down to the temporary stalls that were assembled for the horses that were going to be part of the showcase later. She had spoken to Phillip briefly in the morning on a formal basis, since they were part of the ceremonies and needed to stay focused on what they had to accomplish with their speeches.

She walked up to a magnificent chestnut stallion. The horse threw back its head and whinnied. Shelbi laughed and said, "Yes, Rascal. I know you can't wait to get out and show off in front of all these people."

Rascal and Shelbi became acquainted when he arrived at the farm. She had been part of the group of people who groomed the horses after their travels. Shelbi also had the opportunity to jump on Rascal's broad back and had gone for a brief ride around the green field near the temporary horse stalls.

Shelbi reached out and stroked his forehead. "I know you like it rubbed just here, don't you, Rascal!" she said with a laugh.

She could smell the heavy rich scent that Rascal's coat gave off. It was animalistic and heady. Suddenly, Phillip was in her head.

"Hello, my Shelbi. I see you are with Rascal. You can just feel his hot smooth skin tingling your fingers, can't you? By the way, I had a lonely hot shower last night thinking about you. In fact, I thought of you as I picked up my soap and started to lather my naked body. It did create a certain amount of sexual tension."

A picture of his body leapt into Shelbi's mind. She could see his memory of the hot shower. His hand was lathering his firm stomach muscles then sliding down both sides of his manhood between his thighs. He then gently caressed his manhood as it started to grow and stiffen.

Shelbi's heart started to beat faster as the sexual tension rose to create warmth between the vee of her legs.

"Phillip, it's working. I'm starting to pant, my love."

"Well, my little princess, we will see what happens next!"

Just as suddenly, the prince was gone from her head! Magically, he was standing beside her.

"With the price of grain and the amount Rascal eats per day, we will have to set strict budgets," he said.

Shelbi was stunned. Her head whipped around and she looked at him with questions in her eyes.

He slipped back into her mind with three words, *"Electric purple swirl."*

Shelbi glanced down through her golden lens and sure enough, the electric purple swirls around her thighs had moved up and were rolling around her tummy as well. She immediately focused on the price of grain and responded, "Yes, a budget will definitely be necessary, not only for Rascal, but for all the university's horses."

She leaned her forehead against Rascal's soft brown side, but no matter how she tried, images of Phillip in the shower remained in her mind. She'd have to walk away or this would become truly embarrassing.

"You will just have to learn how to control this better, my prince, or maybe we just shouldn't care!" she said with a laugh.

"Actually, we don't want to get the horses riled, so maybe we just better walk away," he said.

For the rest of the day, when Shelbi was not focused on the events unfolding around her, her mind slipped back to Phillip and wisps of purple rolled up and down her green uniform occasionally. At the end of the day, she got into a hot shower and let her mind roam back to her image of the prince.

"Now I can enjoy you without having to worry about anyone else noticing," she whispered, and she did.

Chapter 15: Waterfall Reward Afternoon

Phillip sat in the wine-coloured leather saddle padding the neck of this dark chestnut horse, Tieyson. His eyes caught sight of Shelbi as she rounded the corner of the stables towards her horse. He focused on the movement of her broad hips as they swung gracefully from side to side. He began to think about peeling those tight beige riding pants off her then kissing the line across the top of her bikini panties until she was panting.

Shelbi emerged from the stall sitting in the saddle of her light brown horse, Rascal. They trotted down the familiar path toward their wonderful crystal clear waterfall and favourite banyan tree. As they reached the pasture near the waterfall, they moved over to the small wooden stable that had been built especially for them. They took the saddles and bridles off the horses so they were free to roam the sweet grasses of the pasture. An invisible fence had been erected so the horses could not walk too far.

As Shelbi approached the shade of the banyan tree, she took out the expanding blanket and dropped it to the ground. She pressed the tab to open it. She walked across to the water and stood looking at the small waterfall beckoning the two of them. She turned around and saw Phillip walking towards her holding a small basket containing some food and water. She sat down on the edge of the soft blanket and felt the warm grass cradle her seat. Then she reached out and pulled her black riding boots and the dark blue socks off.

Phillip sat on the blanket and gently kissed her on her warm full lips then he stood up and smiled.

Shelbi smiled back. "Yes, my love?"

Phillip said nothing but leaned down again and gently caressed her lips. Shelbi smiled again as he stood up.

He leaned down a third time to kiss her as her left hand caressed his neck and slipped her fingers into the hair at the back of his head. Pulling him down, she kissed him harder and held him there as the heat filled her body. Her electric reds and yellows colours were starting. Phillip's hands caressed her backside and he raised her up so he could keep kissing her.

"This is so amazing. If he starts kissing my neck, the warmth will spread even further," she thought.

Phillip thought, *"I just want to kiss her neck gently and arouse the tiger passion I know we have together."*

"Put me down for a moment, my love," Shelbi softly whispered in his ear.

Phillip gently put her feet first on the caramel blanket and saw her take two steps back. She began undoing the buttons of her shirt.

"Just the shirt, I want to help with the rest," he said, sending shivers through Shelbi's body and rolling the red and yellow electric colours faster.

She could feel the warmth building between her legs. The electric purple line was already thinly rising up her tummy. She smiled seductively and looked directly into Phillip's eyes. Phillip sat down and took his riding boots off then moved toward Shelbi.

"Stay right there. I will come to you," he said.

"Yes, my prince. Come for me."

There was so much hidden meaning in that small sentence, but they both clearly understood it.

When he reached her, he began kissing her neck and down her shoulders. Her nipples ached, awaiting the feel of his warm wet lips to encircle them. She wanted his hot tongue flicking and caressing the hardness of her erect pink nipples. The more he kissed the top of her breasts, the harder her nipples became. The electric purple line was swirling around her breasts as his hands gently caressed her arms. His fingers softly roamed down her soft white skin, working their magic and leaving a trail of goose bumps.

The warmth between her eager thighs was hot and turning to liquid. Suddenly, he stood up and undid the buttons of his blue shirt. Shelbi jumped into his strong arms.

"My prince, I want to feel your warm skin on mine!"

She crushed her breasts eagerly against his bare skin and felt the warmth seeping through her blue bra. She ran her fingers gently over his back and could feel the shivers shake his body as he enjoyed the tingling sensation.

She reached behind her and undid her bra, and gently touched her erect hard nipples against his chest. The sensation of her nipples caressing his sweating skin was so enjoyable that it made the heat rush down her breasts across her stomach and through her copper mound to the vee of her core.

"I'm not sure how much of this I can really take," he said with a husky edge to his voice.

"You'll take as much as I give," Shelbi said with a sultry smile.

He began to kiss her milky breasts, took her stiff right nipple between his lips, and breathed warm air on it. Then his kisses travelled across to her left breast and slowly encircled her tented nipple and breathed hot air on it causing it to rise more.

Shelbi shuddered and felt the wetness building between her thighs. The electric purple was swirling around her breasts magnificently. The prince's red and gold electric patterns were overlapping and creating a shimmer around his beautiful manly chest and down his abs.

"You are so magnificent, my love," said Phillip as she removed her tight riding pants.

He ran his right hand between her breasts and down across her flat belly. He continued to run his warm lips over her nipples. He took the edges of her lacy blue panties and gently pulled them down her legs. Shelbi shuddered as the warmth between her naked thighs increased. She knew she was wet and ready for him, but he was not ready to give her that sensational pleasure yet.

Shelbi quickly stepped back so Phillip could take in her beautiful creamy nakedness. The red mound just above her thighs looked so sensational he could barely maintain the his hard throbbing manhood. He reached out.

"No, no, my love, not until you're naked and you touch me again," she said.

Phillip stripped quickly. He had gone commando again and his manhood leapt to attention the moment it was free. She imagined it tucked between her moist thighs, sliding slowly up her hot channel.

He stood up and she embraced him. His erect pulsating manhood was pressing against her belly. Her hands roamed over the skin on his back and down to his beautiful tight ass.

Phillip carefully laid her down on the blanket. As he lay beside her, she swept her right leg over him and ran her fingers across his sweaty chest, amazed at the hard-rippling muscles of his stomach. His fingers trailed down the side of her body and over her broad hips. He slid across the front of her belly to her copper mound and tugged at it playfully. Shelbi was so aroused she had a mini climax. He continued to kiss her neck and caressed her back as she rubbed her erect cherry red nipples across his chest.

Finally, Shelbi could take no more and pushed him on to his back. His hand quickly moved to the top of his manhood and rolled his clear protective sheath down his stiff member.

She straddled him like she had her horse on their way out. Shelbi could feel the tip of his manhood pressing against her vagina. She reached down, grasped his enormous rod, and rubbed it back and forth across her wet pulsating outer lips.

"Slowly, my love, slowly. I want to enjoy every single inch," he said.

"Yes, my love, but as you can see, with all this electric purple swirling around your electric red and gold, I don't know how much longer I can wait!" she panted.

Ever so slowly, she sat on the head of his manhood, pushing slightly in and then moving out. As her body trembled, she began to slowly insert his magnificent manhood, feeling its strength as it slid deeper inside her hot wet channel.

"Oh, you are stretching me and filling me to my core!" Shelbi gasped aloud with pain and pleasure.

The heat between her thighs and the wetness dripped out and slipped down his manhood, making it easier to slide inside her. As she braced herself and began the rhythm of riding him, her breasts swayed back and forth as her hard pink nipples caressed the bare skin of his chest. The electric purple swirled so she could barely see him, except for his golden and red swirls. As the tension mounted, she began to pick up the rhythm.

The tension built suddenly. Her legs squeezed his sides and she plunged down on him, taking him fully inside her. She pulsated in a climax that made her weak and she could barely see the electric purple swirling around. She lay on his chest as she continued to vibrate while her climax slowly ebbed.

Phillip lay still as Shelbi used his sweaty body. He then rolled her on her side and began to kiss and caress her again. Within a few moments, her purple swirl intensified. She began to feel the sexual climax mounting in her legs and moist thighs again.

Phillip's fingers roamed down her belly and found her sensitive clitoris. She knew she was in for another body-shaking climax. His fingers caressed the wetness of her and rubbed her erect nub back and forth. He aroused her more with each circle of his fingers. His warm lips locked on her stiff nipples as he sucked and flicked them mercilessly. Shelbi pushed her breasts into his warm face, feeling the stubble on this chin caressing them.

"Now it's my turn to pleasure myself with your amazing thighs," he said.

Shelbi shuddered with a mini climax at the thought of him bringing her along with his coming climax. She felt the sun caress her body as the beams flicked through the electric purple swirls around her.

He moved his manhood up between her spread legs. His bulbous head touched her tingling clitoris and she shivered again with a mini climax. Then he moved his hips and she could feel him enter her dripping channel. She was slightly sore from being engorged but wanted more. She wanted him deeper.

"My love, you have done your duty for the women of your planet. I also have protection. I really want to feel your nakedness inside me," she said with an urgency Phillip had never heard before.

He slowly pulled out of her and slipped his protection off. Softly, he began pushing in and out, each time going slightly deeper, pushing against the wet walls of her vagina. When Shelbi could take no more, she pressed her heels into his backside to urge him deeper inside her. Their rhythm became one. She could feel his movement inside her as he slid up and down inside her vibrating channel. The ridge on his head pressed against her clitoris and rubbed it hard. The sensation was electric and again the purple swirled around so she could barely see him between the other colours swirling around them.

Finally, his rhythm picked up and, with one final thrust, his warm essence gushed inside her. She felt the flow over and over again. It flooded out of her and down her thighs, mixing with her climax juices. The electric purple almost blinded her. It was the most intense climax she'd ever had. She felt almost exhausted.

"That was a great start, my love," he said with a smile.

"My love, I think I'm consumed. I don't know if I can take much more," Shelbi panted.

"Are you sure?" he said with a sexy sneer.

Shelbi pushed him on to his back, feeling his hardness still inside her. His erection began to move slowly.

"Oh, my goodness. I was kidding. Men get sore too!" he said.

Shelbi just smiled and slowly continued to move over his toned, sweating body.

They spent the rest of the afternoon making love and caressing each other, not worrying about what was going on in the rest of the world. Later, they went down to the cool waters of the river.

As they entered the water, Phillip produced a bar of soap and began to lather Shelbi's back and arms and then started working on her breasts. Shelbi couldn't stand it as the electric purple quickly surrounded them. When he started to soap between her thighs, she felt weak and had to lean against him.

She then grabbed the green soap and started to work on his manhood. She watched it harden and rise. She dove under the water. Phillip quickly followed. He came up underneath her and his tongue played with her sore, stiff clitoris. When he stood up, Shelbi quickly clamped her mouth on the top of his rising manhood. She began to lick it and taste all the droplets that ran down its erect form.

Finally, she simply clung to him. "Please, my love. It's time for us to go back."

They walked out of the water together and dried their naked bodies. As she pulled on her lacy blue panties, she looked at him.

"I truly love it here. I wish we could just stay this way forever," he said with a weary sigh.

"I know, my love, but too many people depend on us. We must go back," she said.

Hand in hand, they walked to the stable and called the horses.

As Shelbi sat in the leather saddle feeling the soreness between her thighs, the electric purple was still swirling around her body.

"I really am going to have to learn how to control this!" she said with a laugh.

"Don't worry, my love. People know exactly what we were doing out here. In fact, they are glad we were together," he said with warmth in his voice.

Shelbi linked to his mind. *"This is the first time I felt that I wanted to stay in one place forever."*

"Wouldn't that be wonderful!"

They thought almost simultaneously, *"I wonder if that's even possible?"*

They wondered what the future held for them. Would they make love at their waterfall again? Only time would tell, and time they both had, for now.

Warrior Alien Passion
The Next Shelbi MacPhadden Passion Adventure!

Chapter 1: A Dirty War Then Soapy Sex

The silver bullets ricocheted dangerously close to her right leg. She threw herself down to the red earth. The pain radiating from slamming her breasts rolled across her chest. She could not fail! Shelbi had come too far to lose it all now.

The two soldiers that had followed her into this potential death trap also lay prone on the hard earth. She was their leader and they would follow her, even if it meant their premature death. Soon, three of her squad would die. That was part of her plan and necessary if she was going to win the war.

Shelbi and her companions shimmied along the dry dirt floor of the battle field, thankful they had covered the metallic parts of their war uniforms so no reflection would be a target for dreaded enemy snipers.

At the planned moment, Shelbi broke radio silence and said one word, "Butterfly!"

Seconds later, three of her squad had jumped up, arms spread like butterflies with their gun laser beams ricocheting out across the landscape. Now they lay dead on the hard earth, mortally wounded by the enemy's return fire.

Before the firing subsided, Shelbi and her two companions slipped up on the enemy squad, pinning them down with their rifles. Then bang, bang, bang. Three bullets. Three dead enemy soldiers.

Each of Shelbi's remaining squad reached out and took a blue armband off the dead soldiers. They slipped them over their green armbands.

Now for the second stage of Shelbi's strategic battle attack plan.

They walked into the enemy's camp near the medical tent. As Shelbi expected, a waiting ambulance sat with its motor running, but with no one inside. Shelbi opened the door and jumped into the driver's seat. One team soldier jumped into the passenger side and one leapt into the empty stretcher in the back.

Moving out quickly, Shelbi drove the ambulance soundlessly through the war zone. As they rounded the corner on the road to the major's tent, Shelbi flipped the switch on the ambulance's flashing red lights.

As she had planned and hoped, when they drove up to the guards posted at the gate, they automatically opened it and the ambulance was waved through. No identification necessary.

They pulled up to the major's command centre, parked the ambulance, and left it running. They moved inside quickly with their rifles at parade rest. As they entered the major's building, they took off the blue armbands leaving the green ones exposed.

Shelbi expected no one would notice. They moved quickly down the grey corridors and into the major's command centre. Again, three helmeted warriors walked forward and no one challenged them. Moments later, Shelbi was elbow to elbow with the major with her gun pointed at him. Her two companions were tight behind, using their arms to lock themselves together, as they pressed against her back.

Shelbi spoke softly, "Major, surrender or die!"

The major spoke one word, "Brittle!"

Guns blazed and Shelbi's two companions were frozen on the spot. The umpire drone pronounced them dead.

Shelbi looked at the major again and softly said, "I won't ask you again, Major. Surrender or die!"

The major looked at the two dead companions leaning against Shelbi and realized, *"My stars, the game is over! We will never get a shot at her without her taking me out. Nothing left but to gracefully surrender."*

He laughed heartily. His left hand reached down and flipped the protective cover off the red surrender scanner patch. His left thumbprint on the glass patch was recognized. The umpire drones noted the strategic action he was taking and his unconditional surrender.

The War Games Umpire system immediately locked down all rifles and guns in the war zone. All the warriors who had been frozen and pronounced dead had their battle suits unfrozen and were free to move.

The major turned and looked at Shelbi. With a slight smile on his weathered face, he said, "Private Shelbi, it would be my honour to have lunch with you tomorrow and discover just what's going on in that head of yours. After 12 cycles, 12 wars, I've never even been close to surrendering. You managed to capture me with only three privates!"

Shelbi took off her helmet and looked at the major.

"Sir, it would be my privilege to have lunch with you. I may or may not divulge my strategy, but I can give you some ideas on how I came up with it."

Again, the major laughed. "Well done, Private Shelbi," he exclaimed to the room. Then he began to clap and the entire room clapped for the three privates that had taken down Major Jackson Eric Sanderson, leader of the blue squad.

As Private Shelbi MacPhadden travelled back to the green squad command centre, she thought back to how she became part of the empire's warrior elite program.

The empire had specifically created the warrior princess group for women to be the military strategic elite but also relationship builders between Earth and new planets they uncovered as they expanded through the universe.

She'd liked growing up on Earth and playing with toys. As her body grew, she began to play more competitive games with girls and boys. Those games used computers and special military war games. She liked the action and feeling like she was part of the games.

By the time Shelbi was 13, her parents had a special space uniform moulded just for her. They had it adjusted as she grew through her teenage years. It fitted tightly to her body as it expanded to fit her broader hips and her growing breasts.

Then she began playing war games outdoors, not just computer simulations: roaming over the land, capturing the enemy, and taking their fort. Being a leader, shooting to kill.

Shelbi's first application for warrior princess was accepted gratefully by the tall athletic female empire warrior scout who had been tracking her progress. Most candidates were rejected on their first application. The Empire Warrior Princess Academy wanted to make sure that their candidates really understood what they were applying for and not just following a fad.

Major Reneey Weatherson, the empire warrior scout, had tracked Shelbi for a number of years. She was fully aware of Shelbi's hidden talents and that she really wanted this military career. After a lengthy review of Major Reneey Weatherson's scout report and the unusual recommendation, the warrior princesses elite application committee had awarded Shelbi the honour of joining the empire's warrior princess elite program at the academy three months after her 19th birthday, just months after becoming eligible.

Shelbi arrived back at the barracks having been transported by the blue squad major's second in command. As the three victorious privates emerged from the armoured vehicle and began to walk into the building, the green squadron formed a line for her to walk down as they clapped and cheered. The green squad had never won a major battle against the blue squad. Now they won both the battle and the war.

Shelbi peeled off to walk towards her living quarters. As she walked down the grey green corridor, Brendenn, a bully she would like to decapitate, emerged from an adjoining corridor.

"Great job, Shelbi. You're lucky, squirt," Brendenn said with a smirk on his handsome face.

Then, as usual, he reached down and grabbed her right ass cheek, lifting her up on her own toes. He laughed and walked quickly away with his three companions.

Shelbi was instantly fuming. She turned and yelled out, "Someday, Brendenn, you lizard, I will take you down hard!"

The very first time she saw Brendenn Corzann, he had turned around and grabbed her ass. He had done the same thing ever since. He was one year ahead of her and knew more about fighting and one-on-one combat than she did. She had signed up just recently for extra training on one-on-one combat and she was going to get him. A smile crossed her face when she thought of his pain as he lay face down on the hard corridor floor.

It'd been a long day of fighting and Shelbi was tired, but she knew she had to go to the victory dinner. As a squad leader, she had been promoted and had her own private room with its own shower. She stripped out of her field uniform and put it in the refresher. Then she walked naked into her shower and grabbed the green soap. *"I really need to feel the hot water soothing these tense muscles,"* she thought.

As she ran the soap over her tired arms, she began to fantasize about what she would do to Brendenn when she beat him. *"You will wish you never picked on Shelbi MacPhadden, you lizard,"* she thought with a smile creeping across her face.

As the hot water pummelled her breasts, she ran the soap over and around them, washing off the dirt, sweat, and grime. The more she lathered her grapefruit sized breasts, the more her red nipples began to tingle and harden. She began to imagine Brendenn taking the soap from her hands and gently caressing her soft breasts and sucking on her tense nipples. She began to flick her fingers over each pulsating nipple, imagining his tongue moving back and forth on each one sensually.

The tension began to rise as she thought of him standing in front of her naked. She could practically see the water running down his chiselled abs. She knew, at six foot five, he would tower over her and the very thought of his naked muscular body sent shivers down her spine. She decided to enjoy playing with herself.

She closed her eyes and began to imagine his fingers running down the inside of her thighs with the soap.

Then she began to think of taking charge. "Drop the soap, Brendenn," she imagined herself saying. Then she thought, *"I'll turn him around and I'll slap his ass hard."*

She began to imagine soaping her soft breasts then running them up and down his bare slippery back, the solid muscles caressing her breasts and tickling her nipples. Shelbi imagined commanding him, "Put your arms to your side and leave them there now!" She could then reach around the front of his naked body and soap between his legs and around his hardening rod.

She could imagine the wonderful length and enormous thickness as she ran her soapy hands up and down his long shaft.

Her hand-to-hand combat was getting better and she knew one day she would surprise him and take him down, regardless of his three companions that always seemed to be with him.

As she towelled the water droplets off her body, she realized she hadn't satisfied herself. She would definitely have to take care of those feelings after the victory dinner. The wetness between her thighs told her that was a necessity. As she dried off her copper mound, the towel flicked against her erect bud.

She turned and flung herself on the bed. *"Why wait for later?"* she thought.

Her right hand began softly caressing the inside of her warm thighs. Her forefinger and thumb found her erect clitoris between the vee in her outstretched legs and began the rhythmic dance of caressing it and rubbing it faster and faster.

"Oh, this is just the sexy reward I need now," she gasped. She plunged a finger inside her wet vagina. Her fingers continued their rhythmic dance on her stiff clitoris as the tension built. Her right hand rose to her breasts, plucked at her nipples, and then back between her thighs riding in and out of her lubricated vagina.

Finally, the rhythm of her left hand over her erect clitoris and her right hand plunging in and out of her sensitive vagina matched the pace she really needed. Clutching her thighs, she began to tremble with that wonderful climax one can achieve when satisfying oneself. As the tremors receded, she slowed the pace of caressing herself.

Finally, she stopped and, holding her breasts, she said, "Well, back to the shower to clean up before the victory dinner."

Looking down at her copper mound, she said, "Yes, dear lips, I'll be back."

To Be Continued . . . .

Look for this next Shelbi MacPhadden, Warrior Princess Elite Adventure, **Warrior Alien Passion** *Kindle book soon on Amazon.*

Shelbi MacPhadden Alien Passion Adventures

Fulfilled Alien Passion
Shelbi MacPhadden Adventure 1

Shelbi MacPhadden is a warrior princess, dispatched to a distant galaxy to make contact with alien species and build relationships with them. Little does she know that her latest mission will test her in ways she could not have foreseen.

Landing on the beautifully lush and tropical planet of Egnaro, Shelbi is greeted by the inhabitants who are obsessed with large breasts and soon persuade her to augment her own to a mind-blowing 38DD.

As she begins to become accepted by the tribe, Shelbi finds herself attracted to Parnell Mahon, a wealthy local businessman. He, in turn, tries to seduce her but she fends him off as she has more important work to deal with.

But, how long can she keep her feelings and needs under control? With her desire mounting, she goes to Parnell's home one sultry evening. Shelbi MacPhadden is intent on making this a night to remember, for both of them.

Desert Alien Passion
Shelbi MacPhadden Adventure 2

Shelbi MacPhadden is an elite warrior and a liaison officer for distant worlds. She enjoys her adventurous career and the sensuous encounters she has with those who inhabit the far-flung reaches of space.

Sent out into a new galaxy, just recently discovered, she lands on the hot and arid planet of Tresed and encounters a group who survive amidst the harshness of their desert surroundings.

Among them is Lance Hopkins, a wealthy businessman with a sumptuous home. Shelbi is immediately attracted to him and something is rekindled in Lance, who has not been in a physical relationship since his wife was tragically killed.

As the two get to know one another, Lance suggests that she participates in a game of the local sport of Z0-Zo ball while Shelbi fantasises about what she will allow Lance to do to her once the game is over. But in the background a sinister enemy plots to have Lance eliminated once and for all.

In the heat of the desert planet it's not just the temperature that's rising. Can Shelbi manage to juggle all her obligations, win the game, save the day and still get her man into bed?

About Sharon Barrington

Sharon Barrington started writing for fun and wanted to share it. Her books are for you, if you enjoy science fiction adventures on distant planets, combined with sexy, romantic passion with strong, naked alien men.

For other Shelbi MacPhadden adventures or to be notified when new releases come out, please go to her Amazon author page, https://www.amazon.com/Sharon-Barrington/e/B07JBQ6DHZ/

Sharon really thanks all those who leave reviews. They really help share Shelbi's wonderful romantic alien passion adventures with others.

Enjoy your own personal passion!

Sharon Barrington